EVERNIGHT PUBLISHING ®

www.evernightpublishing.com

FALLEN GLIDERS MC: VOLUME ONE

Fallen Gliders MC, 1

Lynn Burke

Copyright © 2018

Mel

For a Tuesday night, my little hole-in-the-wall bar in the sticks of New Hampshire hopped. I'd poured countless mugs of locally brewed beer, and seven o'clock hadn't even hit yet. A smile on my face and a bounce in my step because of the country oldies jingling from the new Bose system I'd installed, I greeted most of the patrons by name. Easily done when less than a thousand called the town surrounding the bar home.

I'd always been good with names and faces, though. Came from growing up in the business—in the same brick building with wide plank floors I'd inherited from Grandpop a year earlier after he'd passed. Mom didn't want the place. Never had. She'd always been too busy with her book groups and library volunteering to join her father and me.

A twenty-eight-year-old college dropout, and I made more than enough to keep myself comfortable. And

God, did I love the business. Chatting it up with people, being that shoulder some cried on, that ear others needed to unload in. And living in Grandpop's place above the bar meant I only had to fill my gas tank once every couple of weeks.

"Hey, Janie." I greeted the forty-something woman—the only lawyer in town—who plopped onto one of the few empty stools in the middle of the bar spanning the room. "How's it going?"

"Ugh." She grimaced and dropped her purse onto the bar. "I need a drink."

"Usual?" I asked, grabbing a tumbler.

"Better make it a double."

Still smiling, I poured two fingers of single-malt Scotch and passed it over to her. "Bad day, I take it?"

Janie shook her head, handed me a twenty, and sipped her drink. "Can't wait until I'm sixty-five and can retire. Some people…" She sipped again.

"Kelly's in the kitchen tonight. Can I get you something to eat?" I asked as the bell over the door tinkled, letting me know yet another person needed something to warm their bones on the chilly, damp spring night.

Janie glanced at the entrance, her brow raising. "Damn. I'd take a piece of *that* to chew on for a while."

I turned.

Thick, dark hair shot through with gray and a full, matching beard, unzipped black leather jacket hugging broad shoulders, a trim waist, long legs, and big bulge encased in matching black leathers. My attention traveled back up the tall drink of water, and our gazes collided. His piercing blue eyes seemed to glow in the dimmed overhead lighting, flaying open my skin and baring my soul.

My heartbeat kicked up a few notches, and I

wiped suddenly damp palms down my jeans. Swallowing, I forced my attention back to Janie. She, too, stared at the stranger.

"Hmm," Janie mused, while peering at him. "On second thought, he's a little too old for my taste." She lifted her glass again while continuing to eye-fuck him.

Perfect for mine, I thought while taking another peek at the stranger. My friend Kelly suggested I went for the older men because I never had a father figure other than Grandpop in my life. She said I just wanted a sugar daddy.

If she'd only listen to me when I told her older men were the shit and to give them a shot, she'd be hooked same as me.

The man scanned the room, then strode between the tables lining the far wall and the bar I stood behind, drawing more than one patron's attention. Well over six feet, broad, and in leathers, never mind hot as hell, how could he not draw attention?

A bad boy, I decided as I scrutinized him again. Trouble, if the inked "67" on his neck meant what I thought it did—Fallen Gliders MC. Thank God Sheriff Elliott hadn't stopped in for his usual off-the-clock beer.

The stranger settled onto the only empty stool at the bar's end where he would have a good view of the entire place.

Smiling easily, as usual, I started his way. That blue-eyed gaze found mine again, and God help the tiny strip of cotton inside my panties, because the intensity in his bright eyes turned me the hell on. His attention slipped down over my long-sleeve t-shirt, tightening my nipples, all the way down my tight jeans to my low-heeled boots and back up again. One of his eyebrows cocked in obvious invitation as I drew up before him.

Forget whatever trouble he might bring. I wanted

a taste if he offered.

Time to get my flirt on.

"What can I get ya?" I asked, my voice a little more breathy than usual. On purpose, of course.

"Whiskey. The good stuff." The deep, husky timbre of his voice sent shivers down my spine.

I'd been hoping for a pickup line or downright invitation to fuck like the lust in his eyes told me he wanted, but the night was young.

"Just passing through?" I asked while setting his drink in front of him and keeping the bottle close. He seemed the type to have more than just one.

He didn't answer, but tipped back his head and swallowed the liquor down. "Another," he said, holding out the glass.

A man of few words. I was good with that as long as he knew what to do with the huge cock bulging his leathers.

Our fingers brushed as I took the glass, sending a shock wave straight to my pussy. My clit throbbed, and I fought to keep my hands from shaking while pouring.

His Adam's apple bobbed as he downed that one, and I stared as he licked a droplet of whiskey off his lower lip. On the fuller side, I noted, sure as shit his kiss alone would make me come harder than I ever had before.

"New to town," he finally answered while handing me the glass and motioning with his chin toward the bottle in my hand.

A shiver swept down my skin over the fact he would become a regular. With his love for whiskey and the next closest bar a good five miles away...

Hall-a-freakin'-lujah.

"Melody Hughes, owner and operator," I said, holding out my hand, "but everyone calls me Mel."

His warm hand clasped mine, and my pulse thrummed with energy and the desire to strip down and ride him hard until he shouted my name.

"Dominic Landon, but you can call me Nicky." He released my hand but continued to stare into my eyes. "I'm Ellen Jacobson's brother."

"Shit." I set the whiskey bottle beside the shot I'd poured, expecting he'd be making love to it all night long or at least until I closed down at midnight. "Sorry for your loss."

"Thanks." Rather than down the third, he leaned forward onto the bar, crossing his arms and tightening the leather across his shoulders. "You always this busy?"

I glanced down the length of the bar. Janie winked at me, returning my smile. "Not on a Tuesday, no." Figuring the guy wasn't on the prowl for pussy, having just lost his sister, I put back on my business, friendly face. "Can I get you something to eat? My friend Kelly makes a mean burger."

"Nah. Whiskey's good."

"Well, if you need anything, just let me know." I turned away to attend the other patrons even though I didn't want to.

"What's up with the fine biker?" Janie asked a few minutes later when she flagged me down for a refill.

"Ellen's brother."

"Oh." All trace of interest faded from her hazel eyes. "Poor guy."

"Yeah." I glanced down the bar to find Nicky's gaze on me. I tossed him a flirty smirk and turned back to Janie. "Said he's new in town."

"Sounds like he's planning on staying, then."

I shrugged. "You know me. I don't pry too much. Just listen."

"Guess he'll be stopping in to see me soon."

"Ellen was your client?"

"Along with just about everyone else in this town."

Old Toothless lifted his empty glass at the other end, and I moved his way. Junior Lithgow enjoyed the locally-brewed farmhouse ale. Said the peppery hops kept his sinuses clear. More information than I needed, but he tipped like no one else. Also told stories like no one else. The oldest resident in town at ninety-six, Junior knew everyone and everything. His house also sat alongside Ellen Jacobson's place.

"See Ellen's brother finally made it into town," he mumbled, his words only slightly slurred.

"You know him?" I asked.

"Looks just like their father, God rest his soul. Been wondering how long it'd take him to come back here and try to take everything from young Suzie."

Ellen's daughter, a few years older than me, but I knew her from our high school years. Wrong side of the tracks girl—not that we had a railroad going through town or that one side was really any richer than the other. Her father had disappeared over ten years earlier, the case stalled out with absolutely no leads. Her mother—Nicky's sister—had been a meth addict who overdosed the week before.

"Suzie inherited the place," I said, repeating what I'd heard from Janie.

"That man's no good." Junior leaned forward, his watery eyes taking in our town's newest resident at the other end of the bar. "Steer clear of him, young lady."

Like hell, I will. "No good, huh?" I asked, giving the bar in front of him a quick swipe with a rag.

"Motorcycle gangs, drugs, and women. He's not the kind of man who'll settle down and make any lady happy."

Might make a horny one happy for an hour or so, I thought as Old Toothless continued to prattle on about young bucks and how his generation was the last one to show respect to their elders.

I breathed a sigh when someone called for another drink.

Ellen's brother nursed another two shots before heading out without a word. He left a hundred on the bar, and I hoped like hell he'd be back, because my stash of dildos and vibrators, I had a feeling, wouldn't satisfy.

Nicky

One bar in town, and it had to be owned by a fine woman much too young for me. A bold one who knew her mind, she'd held nothing back from her eyes when checking me out. Probably an easy lay, and fuck, did I need it. I should have stuck around until she closed up for the night, but my feet had grown restless knowing what I'd come into town to do.

My only sibling had overdosed the week before, and probably on the shit my former brothers distributed throughout central New Hampshire. Had I known Ellen had taken up meth, I'd have handed in my colors much earlier than that morning.

I felt bare riding my Harley without the sleeveless vest that labeled me a Sergeant-at-Arms in the Fallen Gliders. Their symbols inked my skin, though, permanent markers of a life I'd decided to give up after thirty years. The "67" on my neck and the FG logo, a chopper with devil horns for handlebars tattooed in the center of my back, lay directly beneath where the logo patch on my vest had been.

Loyalty to the club had always come first—had been a requirement—family and job secondary. Luckily for me, I'd never gotten tied down to an old lady, and my job was the brotherhood. Or, it had been.

I'd stopped by my sister's, now my niece Suzie's place, when riding into town a couple hours earlier, but she'd cursed me through the door and ordered me off the premises. The drinks at Mel's calmed me the fuck down, and I headed back to Suzie's place to try again.

I cut the Harley's engine and hunkered my shoulders against the light mist falling from the dark sky. A lone streetlight tried to cast out a halo of light but failed miserably.

"I told you to get lost!" Suzie screamed through the door before I even finished knocking. "It's your fault!"

"I had nothing to do with her death," I said—again—my eyes closed and forehead resting on the door. "Please, Suzie, can I just come in so we can talk?"

"You're a drug dealer who wanted nothing to do with us, and now that she's dead, you think you can just come in here and stake a claim on what's mine?"

I glanced around the unkempt lawn I could just barely make out in the darkness and paint peeling off the house's siding alongside the door. "I'm not going to try to take anything away from you." Didn't want it. Had no need for it.

"You're full of shit!" Suzie's voice broke, leaning more toward hysterics than sobs. "Fucking loser! Asshole!"

It seemed that Ellen had made sure her daughter thought the same of me as she had for the past ten years.

All because she'd suspected I had taken out her abusive husband, so he would never touch her again. The bastard had simply disappeared one day, never to return. I'd taken care of him all right, but only a select few in the brotherhood knew.

"If you don't fucking leave right now, I'm calling the cops!" Suzie shrieked, and I realized I fought a losing battle.

I stepped off the stoop and climbed back on my bike, figuring I'd try a different day. Even wet and cold, the seat cradled my ass as it had for the past twenty-plus years, offering comfort where there wasn't much. No home or place I'd buried roots except for the club I'd walked out of that morning, vowing to leave that life behind.

Suzie watched me through a window. She hated me, but she was the only family I had left. And if the rumors held true, she'd taken up meth along with her mom. I wasn't about to let anything happen to her.

"I'm not going anywhere," I muttered into the mist. "This town is going to be mine just as much as yours, Suzaroo." The childhood pet name I'd graced her with stung my eyes. How long had it been since those days when Ellen still wanted me around? The days when she was clean. Even if she hadn't been happy with her asshole husband, she'd welcomed me without judgment anytime I happened to stop by.

My town, I thought as the mist turned to rain, pelting my head and the ground around me.

I glanced down the narrow lane leading back to the main road—if you could really call it that. There wasn't even a single red light in town. A handful of random stop signs, and not much else, but I'd known the second I drove downtown that I wanted to stay for the foreseeable future.

I'd booked a room at the only place available, a bed and breakfast which was off the beaten path a good twenty minutes back to the south. Not yet ready to crash for the night, I considered my options. The town didn't have much, but they did have a well-kept bar with decent whiskey. I sure as hell could use a little more burn to warm myself against the chilly rain falling on me.

The old-fashioned bell rang overhead when I stepped through the bar's door less than five minutes later, water dripping off my leathers onto the scarred wooden planks beneath my boots.

Mel glanced up, her whiskey-colored eyes snagging and holding me captive. Too damn fine to ignore. I moved back to the stool I'd vacated earlier and slumped down.

"You're back," Mel said, approaching me with a tempting sway and easy-going smile. Like a beam of sunlight, she damn near lit up the dark shadow that I never noticed I lived beneath.

If I could've remembered how to smile, I'd have given her one in return. "Too early to call it a night just yet," I said, nodding at the whiskey bottle she held up in offering.

Mel poured me a shot, set the bottle beside the glass, and peered into my eyes.

The country music cranking overhead faded, and my cock stirred to life for the first time in a long fucking time. I breathed deep, dying to catch whatever scent clung to her creamy skin, but burgers and booze flooded my nose.

"I'm not usually nosy…" Her voice trailed off, and she bit the inside of her lower lip.

"But?"

"You're in town to settle your sister's affairs?" Mel asked, her voice low.

I decided on honesty since I sure as shit had nothing to lose. "They've been settled. I just want a relationship with the only family I have left."

Mel studied me a little longer, her long, black lashes twitching every few seconds when blinking. Not a stitch of makeup, but her eyes stood out with their pale brown color. Pink stained her cheeks along with a spattering of freckles, and her full lips had me wanting to shove my cock between them and shoot my cum down her throat.

Too damn young.

A master of control, I fought back the urge to clear my throat and adjust my swelling cock. I tilted my head back and enjoyed the whiskey burn down my throat.

"I've heard Suzie is pretty shaken up over her mom's passing."

I poured myself another. "Seems to be, yeah."

Mel's gaze lowered to the tattoo on the side of my neck.

"You know what it means?" I asked while turning my head to the side so she'd get a better look.

She nodded. "Pretty sure Sheriff Elliott down at the other end knows, too."

I glanced down the bar to find a man a dozen or so years younger than me peering our way. Dark buzz cut, dark eyes. He dipped his head and sipped his beer, letting me know he knew exactly who the hell I was. The glint in his eye promised he'd take care of any trouble I thought to start.

I nodded my head in return, letting him know I didn't plan on stirring up any shit. Leaning forward, I propped my arms on the bar and turned my attention back on Mel. "So you probably know why Suzie doesn't want anything to do with me."

A sad smile lifted Mel's lips. "I think I do, yeah."

"After thirty years with my brothers, I handed in my colors. Just this morning." I don't know where the confession came from. Wasn't usually the sharing type, but Mel was easy to talk to.

"I understand why you would do such a thing." Compassion filled her eyes.

A strange ache twisted through my chest, and I frowned. "I gave up everything to come here, and she won't even talk to me."

"Maybe she just needs some time."

I nodded.

"Mel!" an elderly man at the bar's other end called.

Mel glanced over her shoulder and smiled, her

carefree spirit flowing out of her again like a damn ocean swell. "Be right there, Junior!" She turned back to me. "If there's anything I can do to help, just let me know."

My cock sure as hell could use help getting some relief. It'd been too damn long since I had a woman. Hadn't been one decent enough at the club in the previous couple of months to interest me.

Getting too damn old.

Shot glass in hand, I took in the small but well-kept bar. Patrons ranged from a couple of suits and ties to sweatshirt twenty-somethings. A few had stared at me when I'd come back in, and I knew what they saw. Big, broad, and bad ass, I looked like the type of biker parents warned their daughters about. Whatever assumptions made about me would probably be true. Drug dealer. Murderer.

Used to be, I reminded myself, glancing once more at Sheriff Elliott, who continued to stare at me. That life lay behind me, and while I had no fucking clue what to do with myself outside of the brotherhood, I hoped it would include Suzie.

Mel

Nicky stuck around, enjoying my best bottle of whiskey until a half hour before closing time. He tossed another large bill on the bar and said he'd see me later.

Sighing, I watched him leave, enjoying the leather clinging to his powerful legs, muscular thighs, and round ass perfect for digging my heels into. Warmth skittered across my skin for at least the fiftieth time since first seeing him.

I climbed into bed over an hour later, naked, freshly showered, and still horny as hell. Pussy still soaked and needy, I decided to give my favorite dildo a shot at satisfying me. The largest I had, shaped like a real cock with a massive mushroom head, and it glided deep without any resistance. I groaned, imaging Nicky planking over me, his muscles straining as much as I did toward release.

Full, but lacking.

Better than nothing, I decided, angling the dildo to reach deeper inside of me.

A couple of thrusts, my hips rising to my other hand's fingers rubbing my swollen clit, and I came, but not nearly as hard as I'd expected—or wanted. I panted for breath while relaxing on my bed, pulling the dildo from my body.

Empty, and still wanting.

Dammit.

I hoped Nicky would be back sooner than later.

****

Wednesday, I watched the door like a hawk, hoping and waiting for awareness of a bright, blue-eyed stare to sizzle across my skin. The bell dinged countless times, but no Nicky. I kept my smile in place, though, schmoozing the customers as Grandpop would have said. I got an earful from Mrs. Hanks, the town gossip who enjoyed hanging out as much as Old Toothless, sipping her hot toddies.

Forcing myself to listen at least kept me up to date on who was screwing and who was pregnant—out of wedlock. Knowing the dirt helped me know how to deal with people when they came in looking for a good time or to drown their sorrows.

The sheriff stopped in and asked me about Nicky. While his story wasn't mine to tell, I did inform the sheriff that Nicky had handed in his colors. Figured giving out personal information might save Nicky an unnecessary run-in with the law in our small town.

Disappointment hung on my shoulders as I locked up for the night and crawled into bed. My damn dildo only made the itch for Nicky's cock that much stronger. God, did I want him.

I opened at noon on Thursday and served up a dozen or so burgers for lunch. The sun had finally come out, shining through the front windows. At two, the bar pretty much emptied out, and since it warmed enough to prop open the door for the breeze rustling the new leaves of the red maple out front, I did so.

Breathing deep, I went about the after-lunch cleanup, clearing tables and scrubbing glasses while Kelly cleaned in the back.

The rumble of a bike kicked my heart into pumping double, and my smile widened. Minutes later, the hairs on my arms stood on end, and I turned toward the door.

Nicky stood in the doorway, peering at me.

I smiled. "Hey."

He dipped his head and moved through the room to settle on the same seat he'd occupied a few days earlier.

"What can I get ya?" I asked, sidling up as close as I could with the bar between us, making sure to add a little extra w*hat do you really want* in my eyes.

"If you're still serving lunch, I sure as hell wouldn't mind one of those burgers you offered the other day." The heat in his eyes told me he, too, wanted more than mere food.

"Sure thing. How do you want your burger cooked?"

"Bloody as hell, and a side of fries if you've got 'em," he said, peeling off his leather jacket.

A waft of cologne and male musk emanated from his movements, setting the drool factory in my mouth into full motion. Tatts of skulls, hearts, and vines peeked from beneath the short sleeves of his tight, white t-shirt and made their way down to his wrists.

"Scary son of a bitch, aren't I?" he asked, his low voice flooding my pussy.

I lifted my attention to his eyes again, getting snagged in the lust, and everything else faded around us. "Nope, but you *are* seasoned." I made sure to add a little *and I like it* in my tone.

"Seasoned." He snorted a gruff laugh without smiling. "You mean old."

My smile grew, and I knew my eyes damn near sparkled as I ogled him again until the bar hindered my sight of his lower half. "More like an expensive vintage of wine that needs to be consumed."

A low groan sounded in his chest.

"Whiskey?" I all but purred.

"Leave the bottle."

I poured his first round and sashayed away, the back of my neck tingling. My heart pounded, the flutters in my stomach something I hadn't experienced since

Johnny Johnson had claimed my first kiss back in the sixth grade when playing spin the bottle.

Kelly glanced up at me as I walked through the swinging door behind the middle of the bar. "Damn, woman." One of her darkly-painted eyebrows rose. "Who's got your panties melted to goo?"

I laughed. "That obvious, huh?"

"Oh, yeah."

"That Nicky guy I was telling you about."

Kelly shook her head, long, black ponytail swaying, and grabbed the order I'd jotted down. "Seriously, what the hell is up with you and the older guys?"

"I've told you countless times, they're like a fine wine…" I swung back through the door, leaving her laughing behind me.

"Food'll be right out," I called down to Nicky and grabbed another round of beers for the three guys still sitting at the table near the front window.

The slowest time of the day and I couldn't have been happier. Nicky sat alone at the bar, and once I made sure the other three customers didn't need anything else, I made my way back to him.

Rag in hand, I wiped down the workstation closest to him even though I'd done it twice already. "How are things going?" I asked, unable to stand the silent sexual tension between us.

"Not so good with Suzie, but I found an apartment that'll be available in three weeks."

"Where are you staying now? If you don't mind my asking?"

Nicky twirled the shot glass between two fingers. "Staying down at the B&B a few miles back."

"Greta's place."

He nodded.

"She makes a mean apple pie," I said with a moan.

Nicky cleared his throat. "It's on her dessert menu for tonight."

"Then you'd best save room." I tossed the rag into the sink and figured to hell with acting busy. Wasn't like Grandpop was around anymore to talk about idle hands. I leaned on the bar. "So what do you think about our little town?"

"Quaint." He kicked back his shot and poured another.

"Like your whiskey, do you?"

"Better than water."

Elbow on the bar, I propped my chin in my palm. "Mmm. A little more expensive, though."

Nicky smiled, white teeth flashing and a dimple peeking through his whiskers.

"My God," I murmured, my knees near giving way.

"What?"

"You've got a killer smile."

His lips slowly flat-lined again. "Been a while since I've smiled."

"You ought to do it more often. 'Course"—I straightened—"every single woman between here and Conway will be all over your ass if you do."

Nicky actually chuckled, and my own smile widened. "That's where you're wrong, Mel."

My brows shot up. "How so?"

"My appearance scares most people away."

"I'm not scared."

He stared into my eyes, and I pressed my thighs together. "You should be," he murmured, his voice low enough to rumble my chest.

Oh, damn. An animal shone through his eyes—

and not the fairytale shifter-type. The kind of wildness that would take. Devour, on instinct, without thought. I bit down on my lip, unsure of what to think or say.

The bell tinkled over the door.

"Afternoon, Mel!" Old Toothless called loudly, sinking my heart.

A good fifteen minutes earlier than his daily visit, I noted, glancing at the clock on the wall. "How are ya, Junior?" I asked while forcing a smile and moving toward the other end of the bar.

My oldest customer slowly lowered himself onto the stool he'd more or less owned since I could remember. "Bones aren't aching today," he said with a toothless grin.

I tipped a glass beneath a tap. "Because it's beautiful out."

"Heard tell it's going to cool off over the weekend."

Setting his beer in front of him, I nodded. "Looks like storms will roll in, too."

Junior grumbled for a few minutes about the weather and creaking joints while I made noises of agreement.

Kelly came through the swinging door, and I nodded toward Nicky with my chin. She shot him a quick glance and turned back toward me with a smirk.

She delivered, tossed around her ponytail, and waggled her eyebrows at me before disappearing into the kitchen again.

Old Toothless kept me occupied, and as soon as the early birds came in looking for the soup of the day Kelly made from scratch every Thursday, I made my escape.

"You can't be serious," Kelly said the second I walked through the swinging door for a couple bowls of her lentil and lamb stew.

"I am."

"But he's so old!" she whispered, glancing at the door.

"He can't be more than fifty-two or so," I said with a shrug.

"And you're twenty-eight."

"So?"

"So? He's old enough to be your father."

I loaded bowls onto a tray and glared at her. "I find older men attractive. Alluring."

"You're just wanting a—"

"I am *not* looking for a daddy replacement." Kelly's brow rose, and I picked up the tray. "Just 'cuz you don't find him sexy doesn't mean that he isn't." Lips pursed, I strode back to the bar, delivered the soup, refilled a few drinks, and made my way toward Nicky as he stood.

"Heading out?" I asked, totally bummed we hadn't gotten to chat more.

"For now."

I smiled and a ghost of one twitched his whiskers, but the intensity of his gaze didn't lessen. *Only a matter of time*...

"Heading back south for a couple of days to pack up my shit," he said while pulling on his leather jacket.

"Hurry back."

"Plan on it." Nicky winked, and goddamn, did I nearly swoon.

Nicky

Heading south again didn't sit well, but I needed to get my stuff out of the club. Needed to cut ties and try like fuck to move on. The apartment I'd found wouldn't be available for a little over two weeks, and even though Suzie didn't scream at me through her door anymore, I hadn't been able to get her to open the damn thing. Staying with her wasn't an option.

I'd had to sign out of the B&B before heading back to the club since Greta had booked the room I'd been using, so I had no fucking clue where I'd be crashing until my apartment opened up. Camping out under the stars was fine by me—God knows I'd done it countless times while out touring with my brothers.

Jonny had told me I could keep my stuff in the club for as long as I needed, but I swore spiders crawled down my shirt at the thought of going back to that place. Didn't have a choice, though. I'd found a place—my new town—and I was anxious to get my shit and start the last leg of my life.

The sun shone down on me as I pulled into the club's near-empty lot. I cut the engine and stretched my neck and shoulders, talking the imaginary eight-legged fuckers off my skin.

A deep breath, and I strode toward the entrance and pulled open the door. The scent of tobacco, booze, and sex swept over me along with the eighties music Jonny was too damn fond of.

Hawk lounged on a chair nearby, bottle of beer in one hand, a toothpick between his teeth. His eyes lit up. "Knew you'd be back here, you old fuck."

"Only here to grab my shit."

"Goddamn." He stood and grabbed me in half a

hug, and although I wanted to hate everything about my previous life, I couldn't push one of my best friends away. Too much history. Too much of a bond. "I shouldn't let you in here without your colors, but I don't give a fuck," he said with one last thump on my back and stepping away. "Good to see you back, Nicky."

I nodded, hunched my shoulders, and made my way through the bar area, ignoring the skanks I used to take pleasure in. Not one of them could outshine Mel and her vibrant rays of sun.

Body tense, I knocked on the office door.

"What?" Jonny hollered.

I knew the tone all too well. He had a woman on her knees, sucking him off—or trying to, rather.

"Come on out when you're done!" I turned, but Jonny's curse cut through the overhead music.

"Nicky! Get the fuck in here!"

I hesitated a few seconds, hand on the knob, giving whatever whore tried to please him time to pack her shit—and his—away.

"Now!"

Bossy fucker. I pushed in the door and stepped to the side, letting the blonde with the mascara streaks down her cheeks hurry around me.

Jonny sat back in his chair, yanking up his zipper, his dark-eyed gaze glued to my face. "Fucking waste."

"Wasn't working for you?"

"Nothing fucking works for me these days." He pointed at the chair across from him and adjusted himself through his leathers. "Fuck. We need some new blood in the club, someone who knows how to swallow a cock without gagging."

I nodded, although I couldn't find a single fuck to give.

Jonny peered at me over the desk, his brow

furrowed and eyes troubled. "You here to stay?"

"No."

"God damn this shit to hell." He tossed aside some papers and leaned forward, elbows on the old desk his father used to sit behind. "You and Hawk are the only two brothers I trust my life with."

I didn't bother correcting him that I wasn't his brother anymore—just waited for him to continue.

Lips pursed, he shook his head. "I don't know what the fuck is going on here, but there's trouble. Lots of fucking whispering. A handful of the younger brothers took off, leaving their colors behind yesterday." His voice lowered. "The thought they might have followed you off to start another club crossed my mind."

"I'm too fucking old, too fucking done." I gripped the arms of my chair as a frown dented my brow. "You know better than to entertain such a—"

"I didn't give it a second thought." Jonny sat back and heaved a breath.

"I served under you the last ten years, and your father for twenty before that."

"You're loyal." He nodded, still peering intently at my face.

"Was."

Jonny tilted his head to the side and narrowed his eyes. "Meaning?"

"Meaning that I'm done here, just like I told you a few days ago when I handed in my colors." I forced my grip to relax but didn't break eye contact. "I'm loyal in that I won't rat out or give up any shit to the law if that's what you're thinking."

He slowly nodded and slumped back in his chair. "I need a fucking vacation." Pressing the heels of his palms against his eyes, he tipped his head back. "This fucking place… Goddammit."

I opened my mouth, ready to tell him about the perfect hole-in-the-wall bar up Route 16, but clamped my lips shut. Leaving the brotherhood meant leaving my friends behind. Moving on. While I wanted to give a fuck about Jonny, Hawk, and the handful of others I'd considered friends, I told myself I couldn't do it.

Fucking sucked, but Suzaroo needed me—even if she didn't want me.

I stood, and Jonny tipped his head down, the resignation in his eyes like a knife to my gut. "Need help packing up your stuff?" he asked, his voice void of emotion.

"Don't have a lot." Didn't have jack shit beyond my clothes and a few odds and ends from over the years. Trinkets from here and there littered my apartment on the club's second floor, worthless shit since the Gliders lay in my past.

Jonny nodded, seeming to deflate even further into his chair while pulling open the top desk drawer. My keys clinked as he tossed them to me.

I caught them and dropped my hand to my side. "Thanks for letting me keep my truck out back."

"Anything you need," he said, standing and moving around his desk. "Anytime you need it."

My throat tightened, and I dipped my head. "Appreciate it."

"Come on." Jonny clasped my shoulder and turned me toward the door. "The least I can do is carry a bin or two. Stick around for a drink after?"

Hawk grinned at me and tipped his beer my way as Jonny and I walked out of the office.

My mouth watered for a shot or two. I nodded. "One last drink."

****

Done, I told myself an hour later as I pulled out

of the club's parking lot, *never to return.* Hands washed of that life and everything associated with it—except for my Harley on the trailer behind me. Wouldn't ever give her up.

More than anything, I wanted to head north, settle on my new bar stool and drink in the sight of Mel and her bright smile. Her twinkling eyes. The curves of her ass I wanted to sink my cock into.

Too damn young rang in my head more times than I could count, but every time my head whispered the words, they held less meaning. Who gave a fuck if she was easily twenty years my junior? Her body language told me she wanted me. I wanted her with a need that bordered on obsession. Just the thought of her hardened my cock, something that happened on an hourly basis, same as when I'd been a young, clueless fuck of sixteen.

I crashed at a motel a few miles away and took the next couple of days to put the rest of my shit in order, antsy as hell to get back to Mel. Cashed out some investments I didn't want to be associated with anymore. Closed out two of my three bank accounts. Spent a few hours in the pawn shop unloading things I didn't have need of anymore.

Sunday night found me pulling my truck and trailer into Mel's. I'd jerked off countless times to thoughts of her ass, but the release my hand gave didn't offer what I wanted.

Light rain fell, coating my hair before I made it through her door.

Like a magnetic pull, my attention went directly to her, and she turned. Her cheeks flushed and lips parted with a wide smile, and an ache zinged through my chest.

Fucking ray of sunshine.

The bar was packed, but I was able to snag a stool near the one I'd claimed the week before.

"Nicky," Mel greeted me over the blasting country music, her voice breathy and lust-filled.

My cock swelled, and I bit back a groan. "Mel."

"Whiskey?"

"The good stuff." I ran a hand through my wet hair while she grabbed a bottle and shot glass. "Thanks," I said as she poured.

"Good to see you back here."

"Is it?"

My question tipped her head up, and her smile faded. "Yes."

"Mel!" someone called, but it took her a few seconds to turn away, breaking the crackling need to fuck between us.

I downed a couple of shots, ignoring the people around me, focusing on Mel as she worked the bar and the people paying her bills. She had a gift for listening, drawing out people's stories without seeming to pry.

I'd never been so damn comfortable—except for my throbbing cock—in years. Even the club back in the day hadn't afforded me the level of contentment Mel's place did. Glancing around, I decided the stool I claimed again two hours later would be my seat until I breathed my last breath.

Good old Sheriff Elliott climbed off his stool at the other end when the one beside me opened up.

I kept my attention on my shot glass as he took a seat too close for my liking.

"Been meaning to welcome you to our town, Mr. Landon," he said, his tone decent enough but stern as he held out his hand.

Shaking his hand, I nodded, noting the caution in his dark eyes. "Thought you'd come see me sooner or later."

He released his grip. "Sorry about your sister."

Lips pursed, I nodded again and picked up my glass, my gaze flitting to Mel. Concern etched her brow.

"We have a major epidemic in this state," the sheriff said while I swallowed the whiskey.

I kept my mouth shut and poured another shot.

"Mel tells me you handed in your colors, Mr. Landon," Sheriff Elliott continued when I didn't comment.

My gaze trailed after her as she turned away from us to pour another beer for someone a few feet away. "I did."

"Reforming your ways?"

I shrugged. "Not looking for any trouble, if that's what you're asking."

Sheriff Elliott turned on his stool to face me. "I'm more interested in whether you'd consider being a bad boy turned good."

Brows lifted, I peered at him. "What exactly are you getting at, Sheriff?"

"I could use some help."

"With?"

"Any information you can toss my way that could help us clean up our state."

I tipped my head back, downing my drink. "Can't say I remember too much from my days before arriving here." The heat of his stare licked at my face, but I ignored him, still absorbed by Mel and every move she made.

She tossed a flirty smile my way, stirring my cock back to life.

"Well." Sheriff Elliott emptied his beer and threw a twenty onto the bar while standing. "If you decide you'd like to do your part in helping people like your sister, stop by the station."

His words knifed my gut, and I offered one last

nod of feigned indifference. "Nice talking to you, Sheriff."

He left without another word, and I forced my thoughts back to the ass of the bartender and how much I wanted to bury myself balls deep in every hole of her lush body.

Slowly, the place emptied to what appeared to be the regulars, lingering over their drinks and shooting the shit.

"What'd Sheriff Elliott want?" Mel asked after finally making her way back to me.

"Just making sure I'm not going to start any trouble in his town."

"Trouble, huh?" She bit her lip against a growing smirk and glanced at the door. "I didn't hear your bike pull up."

I leaned forward onto the bar, fighting the urge to drop my gaze to her pert rack and the nipples that pebbled anytime she came near me. "That's because it's on a trailer behind my truck along with a couple of plastic bins."

"Better bins than boxes," she said, pointing toward the windows.

Rain fell, and I realized my chances of sleeping under the stars were shot to shit.

"Heading back to Greta's?" she asked while picking up a rag to wipe down the bar beside me.

"She's booked this whole week, which really fucks me up."

"Why's that?"

"Suzie still isn't talking to me, and I've got no place to crash until my apartment here in town opens up."

"Oh."

"Yeah. Any other place you know around here?

Something off the beaten path?"

"Grandpop kept a cot in the back storeroom. Isn't much," she smiled, twisting that ache in my chest again, "but you're welcome to it for the night."

"You mean that even knowing what I am?" I asked, one of my brows raised.

"I know what you *were*." Her smile made the room a little brighter, and she sauntered away, her tight jeans hugging curves that ought to be illegal. Small waist, round ass, and thick as honey thighs my fingers itched to dig into.

I tore my attention from her, cleared my throat, and downed my shot of whiskey. What woman would offer a complete stranger—especially one looking like me—a place to crash? In her storeroom, too? Didn't she notice my love of whiskey? Had she even considered I could rob her blind? Get my hands on her the second the last patron left for the night whether she wanted it or not and fuck her senseless until the sun rose?

A bubbly, seemingly genuinely happy young woman, one who clearly wanted me if the pulse in her neck and poking nipples spoke the truth. Throw the dilated pupils into the mix, and I was ready to bet all the cash in my bank account she'd be up for me bending her over the bar and fucking her tight little pussy. Or ass.

Cock hard and pressing against the confines of the damn leathers I wore, I'd take either. Both. Whatever she wanted, however she wanted it.

Back in the day, she would have been my type. Smiley and sweet, not a drug abusing whore like the rest of the women who hung out at our club. A breath of fresh air, Mel shone like a spotlight in the darkness of my mind, and fuck did I want her.

My cell chimed with an incoming text. I pulled the phone from my jacket.

Jonny: **Wish you hadn't left. Miss you brother.**

I tapped out my reply. **Sorry to leave you and Hawk behind, but it's time I moved on**

Without waiting for his reply, I shut off my cell and tucked it back into the inner pocket of my jacket. I'd told him I was done with a life of distributing drugs that killed. I was done protecting those who delivered, done taking the lives of those who threatened the brotherhood's lucrative business.

I'd been paid, and paid well. I had enough stashed away to last me until a revenge bullet found my brain, or I keeled over an old man. The morbid thoughts lay like a dead weight on my mind. I hoped for the latter, knowing helping Sheriff Elliott in any way would probably lead to a bullet between my eyes. *For Ellen,* my conscience whispered.

"Fuck that," I muttered while pouring another shot.

My attention strayed to the bar's ray of light. A good hard fuck to take away the dreariness sounded a million times better.

Mel

By eleven thirty, the bar cleared out except for Nicky. Rain pounded the windows, and flashes of lightning lit up the dim interior.

Kelly had closed down the grill over an hour earlier, cleaned up our small kitchen, and headed out. I scrubbed the last of the glasses and wiped down the taps with warm, soapy water, all the while warmth and tingles raising the hair on my arms.

Nicky sat nursing the bottle of whiskey. He'd had at least six shots and could damn well hold his liquor.

"How long have you owned the place?" he asked when I finally lowered the music.

"My grandpop left it to me when he passed last year," I said, flipping the two deadbolt locks on the front door.

"Hughsey was your grandfather?"

I shot him a glance, surprised to hear the nickname on his lips. "Yes. You knew him?"

"Used to hang around here back before my sister disowned me and the good Sheriff Elliott took office." He spun his shot glass around in circles on the bar with two fingers as he seemed fond of doing. "Good man, your grandpop."

The familiar ache of loss pinged my chest, and my smile wobbled as I made my way back behind the bar to finish cleaning up. "He was the best."

Nicky scanned the room, no doubt noticing I hadn't changed much of anything since Grandpop's original decorating attempts years earlier. The old brick walls and low timber ceiling lent a cozy feeling that reminded me of Grandpop's warm hugs. Nothing fancy, no TVs. Simply a place to relax and enjoy a drink or two after a long day.

I poured the bucket of dirty water down the drain a few minutes later, wiped my hands on a clean towel, and grabbed a shot glass. Nicky perused me from head to toe and back up again as I rounded the bar and made my way toward him. Delicious shivers swept over my skin, and I sat on the stool beside him.

"May I?" I asked, reaching for the bottle.

He slid his shot glass over while turning on his stool to face me, and I poured us both a round.

"Why did you offer me a place to crash?" he asked, his rumbling timbre tingling between my thighs. "Most people would say you're crazy."

"Probably." I shrugged. "Seems to me that you're starting your life over. Only right of me to help." I held up my shot glass. "To new beginnings?"

"I'm too old for that shit," he grumbled, lifting his glass. "I'll drink to *you*, though."

A rush of pure lust soaked my panties at the want in his blue eyes. "To each other, then." I smiled and clinked my glass against his while crossing my legs to ease the ache in my clit.

We knocked the liquor back, and our gazes met as we set the glasses on the bar.

"How old are you?" Nicky asked, his attention snagging on my lips.

"Twenty-eight."

He scrubbed a hand over the beard lining his jaw while looking away. "So damn young."

"Not *too* young." Gauntlet thrown, I waited for his attention to return to my face. Eyes full of lust, a leashed animal that ought to scare the shit out of me but didn't.

"I'm no good."

I cocked my head and slid my gaze down over

him, not missing the hard length straining against his leathers. "Look pretty damn good to me."

His low groan rushed need through me again, and I knew I'd leave a wet spot on the stool once I got up.

"You're messing with fire, little girl."

Heat flushed through me. "I enjoy flames now and then." My breath caught at the hunger on his face, parting my lips.

"Fuck it." He grasped my chin in his warm palm. "I'll give you what you want, little girl, but don't go crying to your mommy in the morning because a big bad wolf left his mark on you."

Oh, God. I swallowed and squeezed my thighs together. Older men were *so* the shit.

He captured my lips, but without the brute force I'd expected. Hunger, yes, but the full softness of his lips pressed against mine, taking and tasting, his tongue probing, whiskers brushing my skin. I parted my lips and moaned as he sank his tongue into my mouth, fucking every hidden corner, filling me with the taste of whiskey and pure male. My skin pebbled, pulse thrummed.

"Goddamn." Nicky stood and yanked me off the stool. Virile, pure hardness and muscle beneath the leather hiding his skin from my grasping hands. His fingers fisted in my long hair, tangling and yanking my head to the side, the other grabbing my ass and hauling me against his huge cock.

He crouched down slightly and pulled me up. My legs wrapped around him as though having a mind of their own—even though I had been thinking about getting him between my legs all night long.

His beard brushed along my neck as he breathed me in and licked from my collarbone to my ear. "You smell like a fucking spring day. Innocent."

"I'm h-hardly an innocent," I gasped as he bit my

earlobe and ground his cock against my sopping jeans.

"Thank God, because I want to be balls deep inside of you. Now."

He thrust, and I moaned, my fingers grasping at his t-shirt.

"Tell me to stop," he whispered harshly in my ear.

"No way in hell."

With a growl, he squeezed my ass to the point of pain. "I haven't wanted a woman like this in a long fucking time."

"So take what you want."

"Goddamn." He rested his forehead on mine. "Right here?"

I slithered a hand between us to grasp the hardness inside his leathers. "Right now."

"Fuck." Like my five-foot-six frame and thirty extra pounds meant nothing, he spun me around. "Hands on the bar."

I did as told, bending at the waist and putting my ass on display with a little wiggle.

"Don't move," he said while peeling off his leather jacket.

My legs trembled, and I turned my head to watch as he moved to the front door and flicked off the lights.

The streetlight half a block away barely cut through the storm, but the flash of lightning lit Nicky up as he stalked back toward me, shedding his t-shirt.

Broad shoulders … another flash filled my eyes with tanned skin stretched tight over massive pecs and abs a twenty-year-old guy would kill for.

I licked my lips, hoping for another flash of light, but Nicky palmed my waist and leaned over my back, his cock pressed against my ass, the heat of his skin searing me through my shirt.

My eyelids fluttered shut as he wrapped his fingers around my hair again and tilted my head back.

"Last chance, Mel." His rumbling voice and hot breath against my ear brought a moan past my lips.

"Take me," I managed to whisper and licked my dry lips. "Please."

Nicky moved his hands from my hips in toward my belly, releasing the snap of my jeans. Although skin-tight, the jeans were stretchy, and I sucked in my stomach as he slid his hand inside my panties, fingers slipping through my wetness.

"You're fucking soaked."

As though I needed to be told. "*Hurry…*"

The sound of him sucking his fingers clean along with his following groan weakened my knees. "Goddamn, you taste good, little girl."

He kneeled behind me and peeled my jeans and panties down over my thighs. His nose brushed along my ass crack, and he breathed deep. "I'm going to bury my cock balls deep inside of you."

"Yes." I panted the word, so fucking far gone already I knew I'd come the second he pressed into me.

Cursing, he yanked off my boots, and I fumbled to step out of my jeans as he pulled them from my ankles. Naked from the waist down, bent over and grasping the bar … I'd fantasized it over the previous couple of hours but didn't think I'd get so damn lucky.

Thunder boomed outside, rattling the windows.

Eyes still clenched shut, I waited, trembling with need as his zipper sounded. The blessed crinkle of a condom, which hadn't even crossed my mind, reached my ears.

He kicked my feet apart, and I squeaked as he grabbed my hips to keep me from falling over.

One fucking thrust and he filled me to the brink,

shooting my climax up through me with a blinding shriek flying past my lips.

He slammed into me over and over, drawing out my climax as I gushed around his thick cock.

"So fucking tight," he growled, his fingertips digging into my hips. I'd bruise come morning for sure.

The spasms in my pussy lessened, but I continued to pant, clutching the edge of the bar as he thrust into me like the animal I'd expected.

I wanted more.

A flash of lightning lit the bar, and he yanked me back against his chest, holding still. One hand glided down over where we joined, his soaked fingers sliding up to find my clit. He kept his hips still, his cock throbbing deep inside of me. Palming my breast through my shirt with his other hand, his lips and teeth grazed my neck as I squirmed in his hold, trying to get him to fuck me.

"Give me another, little girl." He pinched both my nipple and clit at the same time, and I screamed as another climax tore through me, sending another gush of cum over his cock. My body jerked in his hold, and he squeezed me tight, his hard length buried deep, still unmoving.

"Fuck me," I cried, my nails digging into his forearms. "Please, Nicky. Move!"

He sank his teeth into my neck and he obliged me, pulling out to the head and plowing back into me with a grunt.

I held on for dear life, unable to move even if I'd wanted to as Nicky took what he wanted, his steel-like cock slamming into me, over and over, with a controlled yet wild ferocity I'd never experienced before.

His vise grip squeezed the breath from me. "Fuck!" He hollered and shuddered with release, and for the first time ever, I wished condoms weren't necessary.

I wanted to feel his hot cum shooting deep inside of my pussy.

"Goddamn, Mel," he growled against my neck, his thrusts slowing until he held me still in his arms. "Fuck."

Smiling and limp as a wet noodle, I enjoyed the rush of blood ringing in my ears and euphoric tingles spreading through my limbs.

"Did I hurt you?" Nicky asked, pulling out but still holding me upright.

I'd never felt so damn empty. I smiled and shook my head even though I expected I'd be a little sore come morning. "That was fucking fantastic," I said with a sigh, still smiling. He slowly released me, and I swayed forward, taking two trembling steps to grab the bar. "Holy shit."

"You okay?" he asked.

I slumped on a stool and rested my hot forehead on the cool wood of the bar. "Better than okay. Damn." Unable to move, I sat and listened as he zipped back up and made his way through the darkness to the bathroom a few feet away.

My breathing slowed, and I sighed again.

"Here." Nicky pressed a warm, wet cloth into my hand. "I'll get your panties."

"Add them to your collection," I said with a light laugh as a low rumble from the passing storm rattled the old windows yet again.

"I don't have a collection," Nicky grumbled.

"Surely you jest," I teased. "With a weapon like that, and all those women available to you at your club…"

"The whores at the club didn't interest me much."

"Too bad for them," I said as a shiver rippled over me. "They missed out."

"Want your jeans?"

"Too damn beat to pull them on. I'll just head upstairs like this."

"Upstairs?"

"My apartment. Door and stairs are through the office." I heaved a sigh and forced myself upright. The lack of food since my late lunch left me lightheaded. Although a tad overweight and curvier than I'd have liked, I had no issues walking around naked.

I took my panties and jeans from Nicky, trying to read his face in the dim glow of the streetlight. Backlit, his eyes remained in the shadows. "Why don't you come on upstairs and I'll get you a pillow and blankets for the cot."

"Lead the way."

That damn husky, deep voice... I'd come harder than I ever had—twice—within five minutes, and I wasn't anywhere near sated.

I wiped my smeared cum off the stool before making my way back to the office. My hand fumbled in the dark, but I found the switch and flipped it up. Blinding light squinted my eyes. "Shit, that's bright."

Nicky murmured his agreement behind me while shutting the door. "Damn, woman, you've got one fine ass."

I glanced over my shoulder and wiggled my hips.

Brow raised, he lifted his gaze to my face. "Keep teasing, and I'll be taking that next."

Unable to help myself, I wiggled again just to see what he'd do.

His gaze dropped to my backside, and I stood still as he crowded against me, both hands palming my cheeks. "I ought to spank your ass red for taunting me like that."

"Mmm." I pressed against him.

He stepped back and swatted me. Hard.

With a yelp, I jolted forward, panties and jeans clutched to my chest.

Nicky stared at me with enough lust to melt the most frigid woman. Need revved up again between my thighs, and I squeezed them together.

"You liked that."

"Yes," I replied, my voice breathy.

He groaned, his gaze dropping. "You've got my handprint on your ass, and it looks damn good on you, little girl."

With a come-hither smirk, I turned away and made sure to put a little extra sway in my hips while crossing the office to the door leading upstairs. "Coming?" I asked while pulling the door open.

Another groan was the only answer I got.

Nicky

Mel was unlike any woman I'd met, and I knew, without doubt, she'd be the death of me. Having a heart attack while fucking had to be the best way to go, and if she wanted to push me to that end, I was on board.

I followed her up the creaking stairs, leaning toward her ass and breathing in the scent of her. Sweet, yet musky. I remembered the taste of her, and my cock stirred as though I'd gone back to being a teenager again, insatiable and ready to fuck at the drop of a dime.

She unlocked the door at the top and stepped back, motioning me in. "It isn't much, but it's all mine, rent-free. Make yourself at home while I go clean up."

The tiny kitchen we'd entered gave way to a living room with a faded yet comfortable-looking couch. The coffee and end tables had seen better days, but the TV in the corner was new.

Mel disappeared behind one of two doors, and I sat on the couch, leaning back to ease my cock straining against my leathers. I'd gone pretty hard on her downstairs and didn't want to push, leaving her sore and possibly hesitant about getting with me again, because Christ, did I want her. Every way possible, as often as possible until my legs or heart gave out.

She waltzed into the living room, a silk robe wrapped around her curves.

I whistled. "Tell me you're naked beneath that."

"I'm naked beneath this," she murmured, straddling me.

Grasping her hips and tugging her against my cock, I stared at the hard pebbles I wanted to lick hidden by silk. "You know your mind, don't you?"

"Pretty sure I can read yours, too." Mel slipped

the robe off her shoulders, and I moved forward, closing my mouth around a nipple. With a groan, she slid her fingers through my hair and held me tight against her chest as I nibbled and licked. "Your whiskers feel amazing on my skin," she said, grinding her pussy against me.

I grabbed her ass and kneaded a few times before slipping my hands beneath the silk to her skin. Over and around, I mapped her curves, my fingertips gliding down over her puckered hole.

"I want you, Nicky," she said, pulling my face away from her breasts. "And not just in payment for the bed I'm offering."

Her smile brought a chuckle to my lips, and she stared at my lips as a rare smile curved them.

"You're gorgeous," she said, her hand caressing my whiskered jaw, thumb brushing over my lower lip.

Gray hair, wrinkles at the corners of my eyes … I didn't know what the fuck she saw in me, but I wasn't about to complain. I grasped the back of her head and yanked her down, taking her mouth. Tasting every inch, breathing in her sweet breath, drinking in her light.

"Bedroom," she whispered, the second I let off her mouth.

I held her close and stood up, and she grasped at my biceps.

"Damn, you're ripped…"

"For an old fart," I finished for her while turning toward the only other door in the apartment.

She swatted my shoulder. "I was *not* going to say that."

"Thought it, though."

"Did not."

I pushed in the cracked-open door with my foot, not bothering with light. Enough shone in from the living room that I could make out the queen-sized bed directly in front of me. I tossed her onto the mattress, and she squeaked, her breasts bouncing.

"Take off the robe," I said, struggling to get my boots off.

Mel took her damn time with the knot at her waist before tossing the robe aside. Naked as a fucking jay, she sprawled out, legs spread, propping her upper body on her elbows. Her gaze honed in on my fingers as I unsnapped my leathers and pushed them down.

My cock jutted free, and I wrapped my hand around my length, sliding down to the base. While I wanted to bury myself in the pink glistening heat I stared at between her thighs, I wanted her lips on me.

"To the edge of the bed," I said, holding my cock out toward her.

She scooted toward me without hesitation and sat on the edge of the bed, lifting her attention to my face.

"Suck me."

Leathers still encasing my legs to the knees, I closed the distance between us and tapped the head of my cock against her parted lips.

Her pink tongue flicked out, swiping the bead of pre-cum off me. "Mmm," she moaned, licking again as though hungry for more.

"Open up, little girl."

She opened her mouth and took me deep into her wet heat, her tongue lathing along my length.

"Fuck." Her lips wrapped around me, cheeks hollowing as she sucked, backing off. "Goddamn, Mel." She moved back toward me, and I fought the urge to shove my cock against the back of her throat.

Giving control over wasn't something I did often. Hell, I couldn't remember the last time I'd allowed a woman to suck me on her terms. I normally took what I wanted, how I wanted.

I wrapped my hands in her long, dark hair but allowed her to lead. Lips, tongue, and grazing teeth took me to the edge a hell of a lot faster than I expected. With a groan, I pulled away, her mouth popping off me.

My cock glistened with her saliva, bobbing with the need to bury deep again. Mel stared up at me, her whiskey-brown eyes wide and full of want.

I needed to fuck her face to face, watch her eyes as she came, but I wanted her ass squeezing my cock. Been wanting that very thing since first laying eyes on her generous backside. I'd hoped to get lucky and planned for it.

"Lay back."

Mel did as told, and I yanked off my leathers, pulling the packet of lube and another condom from my pocket.

I crawled between her thighs, and she lifted her hips toward me as I dipped my head down, breathing her musky scent deep into my lungs. Settling onto my stomach, I licked her asshole and up through her sopping pussy. Her tangy sweetness filled my mouth, and I dove in for another long lick, swallowing down every trace of her arousal I could find.

"Oh, my God," she whimpered, her fingernails digging into my scalp and heels digging into my back.

Gaze on her face, I blew across her extended clit and closed my lips over the nub.

Eyelids fluttering shut, she tipped her head back with a deep moan, her thighs squeezing the sides of my head and muffling my hearing.

Better than any damn whiskey, I thought, lapping up the wetness dripping from her pussy. Smooth and addictive.

I kissed my way up over her soft curls, thankful

she didn't shave like women seemed to think all men wanted. Nothing like a real woman, unapologetic in her owning her body in its natural state.

Our lips met in a rush, and she moaned into my mouth, her tongue curling along mine as though getting off on her own taste lingering on mine. I fucking sank beneath the surface of Mel, losing myself in the feel of her soft skin beneath my hands, on my chest, cradling my length as I slid up through her soaked folds.

The temptation to just push right into her tight heat—fuck the condom—rushed through me, and I forced myself to back off, rising to my knees between her thighs. I grabbed the damn condom, rolled it on, and ripped off the top of the lube packet with my teeth.

Mel started to roll over, but I stopped her with a hand on her hip. "I want to see your face when I take your ass."

She licked her lower lip and nodded, pulling her feet up to rest on the mattress beside her ass.

I squirted some lube on my cock and worked myself over a few times. "Have you done this before?" I asked, wanting to know how gentle I needed to be.

"Anal, yes, but not face to face."

"Just relax," I said, smearing the rest of the lube on my fingers, "and tell me to stop if you need me to."

Lower lip between her teeth, she nodded, her head falling back as I rimmed her hole. I slipped one finger past her ring of muscles, pressing in and out, lubing her up good for my throbbing cock.

"Feel good, little girl?" I asked, pressing in deeper.

"God, yes," she groaned, her hands fisting the sheet beneath her.

I pulled out and slid in a second finger. "You're so fucking tight. I can't wait to feel you around my cock."

She gasped as I pressed in as far as I could and rubbed my other thumb over her clit. "I'm going to come."

I backed off and lifted her legs, propping her calves on my shoulders. "Not until I'm balls deep inside this sweet ass like I've been dreaming of since first laying eyes on you." Another groan rose from her chest, and I pushed the tip of my cock against her hole. "Relax..." A slow, easy thrust buried a few inches of my cock in her heat, and I pulled out to the head and pressed back in, gaining another inch or so.

"M-more," she half sobbed, grasping at my biceps as I planked over her.

Jaw clenched, I pulled back and rocked in again and again until my drawn-up balls rested against her skin. "Goddamn." I clenched my eyes shut and breathed, wondering how a woman could make me feel like an inexperienced teenager again. My control slipped, and I shook my head, opening my eyes.

Mel stared up at me, pupils huge, lips parted. She panted, whiskey-laced breath fanning my face.

My chest ached like a motherfucker. Death by fucking, or something else? Needing to get the fuck out of my head, I took her mouth and began moving, my tongue in time with my thrusting cock, slow and drawn out movements. Savoring yet plundering.

Her hips rose to meet me, lifting her backside completely off the bed, and I wrapped my arms around her body, squeezing her legs to her chest. She didn't complain but reached down to grab my hips. I thrust harder. Faster. Her ass welcomed my length, squeezing and enticing me to give over.

Sweat beaded my brow and back. I tore my lips from Mel's and sucked wind as her bed began to squeak beneath us. Every thrust bumped her headboard against her wall and tore a gasp from her lips.

"I n-need…" She licked her lips and attempted to arch her back, but I held her tight.

"You want to come, little girl?" I asked with a deep thrust.

She whimpered and nodded, her nails digging into my ass cheeks.

"Look at me."

Her eyelashes fluttered up, revealing eyes hazed by lust. Passion. Pink flushed her cheeks, making her freckles stand out.

Fucking beautiful.

I backed off enough I could reach between our bodies. I pinched her clit between two fingers, and Mel bucked beneath me with a shriek, her head thrown back, tendons prominent in her neck. Fingernails breaking my skin.

Wetness poured from her pussy down over my cock and balls.

Fucking *mine.*

I closed my eyes and gave over to the orgasm rushing through my body. "Fuck!" I hollered, cum shooting up through my cock, filling the condom, every spurt an explosion of stars behind my eyelids as I thrust like a wild animal. "Fuck," I growled again, my arms shaking as I slowed. Forehead tipped against hers, I fought to catch my breath, amazed my heart still beat.

I started to pull out, but she dug her nails into my ass again. "Not yet."

Allowing myself to relax, I settled onto my elbows and buried my face in her sweaty neck.

Mel

Holy shit.

Euphoric tingles swept over my body like a gentle wave, and I smiled as Nicky's whiskers tickled my neck. A fine wine, I'd compared him to. I held back my snort. More like a Glenfiddich fifty-year-old Scotch only a select few people ever got the privilege of sipping.

Best lay ever, and fuck was I addicted. No way was I about to let him leave me for the damn cot downstairs. I clung to his body, breathing in pure male and the remnants of whatever warm cologne clung to his skin.

A sigh rippled down through me, and my muscles gave way, releasing their hold on Nicky.

His softening cock slipped from my body, leaving me empty yet satisfied. "Be right back," he grumbled, his voice low.

I straightened my legs and winced as he slid off the bed. While gymnastics had been fun in grade school, my body didn't like the idea of bending in ways it wasn't used to. He'd held me down tight as hell, but I'd been too far gone with lust to care about the fact I could have made out with my knees while he fucked my ass.

Snickering, I rested on the mattress that seemed to drain the life right out of me. Eyes closed, buzzing in the afterglow of our fucking, I listened as he cleaned up in the bathroom. A few minutes later, the bed dipped, and he lifted one of my legs.

I reached for the wet cloth in his hand, but he shook his head. "Let me."

I'd never had a man care for me like Nicky did, wiping away every trace of cum from my pussy and lube from my ass. "Did I hurt you?" he asked, setting the washcloth on my bed stand.

"No." I grabbed his forearm and tugged, needing him beside me.

He stretched out, and I rolled to my side to face him.

Sated blue eyes peered into mine, and I ran my fingers along his whiskered jaw, my thumb finding his lower lip, same as before. "Did I hurt *you*?" I finally asked, breaking the stillness between us.

"No." His sweet, whiskey-scented breath brushed over my face, and I leaned up to kiss him.

Languid strokes of our tongues led to a shuddering sigh.

"Best damn fuck of my life," I whispered, finally pulling away.

He smiled, sending an ache through my chest. Dimples. Flashing teeth. Even his eyes twinkled.

"You are so damn hot," I murmured, staring at him.

His chest vibrated against mine as laughter passed his delicious lips. "You drunk?"

"Hell no. Just smitten with our town's newest bad boy resident."

Nicky's smile faded along with the laughter in his eyes. He seemed to retreat inside of himself. "I *am* bad."

"Were."

He heaved a heavy breath and rolled onto his back, staring at my ceiling. "I don't know what the fuck I am anymore. All I've known, all I can remember being is a biker gang member. Fucking drug dealer and protector of my brothers."

I lay my hand on his chest and pressed against his side, soaking in the softness and warmth of his skin. "You've got a blank slate before you. Fill it up however and with whatever the hell you want."

"Knock off a few bucket list items?" he asked without any trace of amusement.

"If you've got one, start it early while you still have time enough to mark them all off."

He turned his head toward me and lifted a hand to tuck strands of my hair behind my ear. "I thought you would be the death of me tonight."

I smiled. "Heart attack while humping?"

The light returned to his eyes. "Death by fucking."

"Didn't work if that was your wish." I kissed a skull on his shoulder. "But you can try again if you want."

"Is that an invitation to stay until morning?" he asked. "Because you wore my old ass out and I don't feel like moving."

"Stay until morning," I whispered, my heart and body telling me I never wanted him to leave.

He continued to peer into my eyes, his expression unreadable.

"What?" I asked.

Lips pursed, he shook his head and ran a knuckle down my cheek.

"Tell me."

"I've never wanted to spend the night with a woman before."

My heart lit up in my chest. "Really?"

"Really. There's something about you that makes it easy for me to relax. Shit." His lips twitched. "I've never done the pillow talk thing, either."

"Same here."

He rolled toward me again, propping his head alongside mine on the pillow I used. "Talk to me."

"About what?" I asked while tucking a hand beneath my cheek.

A light shrug lifted one of his shoulders. "Anything. Everything."

"Okay." I blew a breath between my lips. "I grew up right here in hicksville in a tiny ass apartment with my mom. My dad was a one-night-stand sperm donor twenty-nine years ago, and Mom always claimed I was enough for her. She never married, never had any more kids."

"Did you ever consider trying to find your dad? Did you ever want to?"

"Nope. Never needed him, so why bother? 'Course"—I snickered—"Kelly says I go for older men because of some daddy complex I have."

"So what's the real reason you go for the older men, then?"

"Why drink a cheap wine when the good stuff is aged in oaken barrels to perfection?"

Nicky actually chuckled, widening my smile.

"There's that killer smile again."

Silence settled for a few seconds while we stared at each other.

"So your turn," I said. "Where are you from and all that good stuff?"

"Grew up in Melrose, Mass. Both my parents passed, and Ellen was my only sister. Suzie's the only family I have now that I left the Gliders." A frown flitted across his brow.

"Are you regretting that decision?"

"The only thing I regret is getting involved with them to begin with. I was so caught up in the idea of a brotherhood, putting the club first and all that shit, that I was blinded to the truth of what we were doing. What I condoned and protected."

"It isn't your fault," I said quietly. I'd meant Ellen, and he nodded as though understanding.

"Thank you."

"For what?"

"Listening." He pulled me against him and gently kissed my lips. "And for not kicking me out tonight."

****

A calloused palm roamed my hip and thigh, and I blinked my eyes open as a shiver rippled over my entire body, pebbling my skin. I stretched, arching my back and pressing my ass against the hard cock behind me.

Nicky's low growl and fingers gripping my hip sent a shot of pure lust straight to my pussy. He pressed his chest against my back and pulled me against him with a rough jerk. "I want to fuck you," he said, reaching a hand between my thighs to stroke through my wetness.

"Mmm." I smiled and reached a hand over my shoulder to run my fingers through his thick hair.

Cock pressing against my thigh, Nicky pressed two fingers inside of me with a growl. "Is that a yes?" His rasped morning voice sounded like sin and sex, and I wanted both.

"Yes."

He rolled away, and the crinkling of a condom wrapper sounded before he returned, sliding an arm beneath me and a leg between mine.

I propped my leg over his thigh, and he reached around again, teasing my clit while rubbing his cock through my slickness.

"Tell me you want me inside of you," he said with a groan against my ear, his other hand slipping beneath my body to grasp one of my breasts.

"I want your cock in me."

Nicky thrust, and I gasped, arching at the sudden invasion that left me full and aware of the soreness from the night before.

"Your pussy feels so fucking good squeezing my

cock, little girl." He stopped rubbing my clit and wrapped his arm around my waist to keep me from moving. "I could die a happy man right now."

"Don't you dare." I tried to grind my ass against him. Needed him to move, but he held still, nuzzling my neck, massaging my breast. "Damn sadist," I grumbled, clenching my pussy muscles.

"*So* fucking good." He brushed his hand down over my stomach and flicked my clit.

"Goddammit!"

He flicked again, and my body tried to buck but failed.

"Move!" I gasped as he extended my clit between two of his fingers while plucking my nipple.

"I want you to come around me first. Clench me tight with this sweet pussy." Three quick flicks and my climax rushed over me.

"Christ!" I shrieked as a gush of wetness coated his cock buried still inside of my spasming pussy. "Goddamn you, Nicky! Please!"

With a growl, he pulled out and slammed in over and over, the animal unleashed, drawing out my climax and sending another ripping through me before I caught my breath. His hip bones drilled into my ass with every forceful thrust, his hold on my waist keeping me from moving.

I dug my fingernails into his forearm that rippled and flexed beneath my hold. Like a steel cage, his body held me tight while fucking me with pure ferocity.

"One more." He bit my earlobe. Loosening his hold, he yanked on my nipple and clit at the same time again with enough pull to send shooting pain and pure lust on its heels through my body.

Another shriek tore from my lips, and I arched my back, thrusting my ass toward him.

"So. Fucking. Sexy." Nicky thrust with each word, the head of his cock slamming against my womb. "Fuck!" He squeezed me tight and shuddered, his cock jerking inside of me. "Fuck, Mel." A few more thrusts and he stilled, his arms in a vise clamp around me, face once more buried in my neck.

"I haven't killed you yet," I muttered, completely spent and limp, "but you've wrecked me."

For life.

Tingles continued to roll through my body as our breathing quieted. Nicky loosened his grip and returned to rubbing his hand along my hip and thigh still draped over his.

I didn't want to move, could have been content to stay in bed all day.

"Tell me you have coffee," Nicky grumbled near my ear, his whiskers tickling.

"I have coffee," I said, stroking up his forearm to lace my fingers through his still atop my breast. "You'll have to let go of me, though."

"Don't fucking want to."

A huff of laughter jiggled my breasts, and with a sigh, he released me, his softening cock slipping from my body and leaving me with a heavy emptiness.

His footsteps padded across my floor, and I rolled onto my back, stretching and wincing yet again at the soreness between my thighs. *Damn.* I squeezed my inner muscles, expecting we'd have to take it easy the rest of the day.

"Fuck." Muttering a few more curses, I sat up and pushed my messy hair over my shoulders.

Nicky stood in the bathroom door in all his naked, tattooed glory, long, flaccid cock hanging between his muscular thighs.

"Goddamn, you're fine." I breathed the words,

drinking in my fill.

His stomach muscles tightened, and I groaned as my drool factory roared to life. "Coffee. Yes." I tore my stare from his sinful body and slid off the bed onto wobbly legs. I grabbed my robe, wrapped it around me, and shuffled into the kitchen, trying to ignore the sting between my thighs.

It's like I lost my virginity all over again, I thought while measuring out the grounds. I couldn't imagine losing my virginity to a cock like Nicky's. A shudder rippled through me, and Nicky's presence behind me pebbled my skin.

A smile sprang to my lips, and I glanced over my shoulder. "Good morning."

His dimple made an appearance, and fuck me, did I feel myself falling. "Morning."

God, his morning voice…

My pussy didn't give a damn it'd just been plundered. Warmth lit inside of me, and I shook my head. The worst drug.

Neither of us spoke while the coffee brewed and I pulled mugs from the cabinet. I popped some cinnamon raisin bread Kelly had made into the toaster and grabbed the creamer from the fridge.

"I'm not a big cook," I said, placing the toast and butter on the table a minute or so later. "Thank God for best friends who can."

Although Nicky's smile had diminished, the light in his eyes remained as he watched me putter around the kitchen, pouring our coffee. He mumbled his thanks when I placed a steaming mug in front of him.

"So." I sat and wrapped my hands around my coffee cup. "What are your plans?"

His brow rose as he lifted his mug. "For?" He sipped and rumbled appreciation. "Good coffee."

"Thanks." I smiled and sipped. "What were you planning on doing for work?"

He shrugged and took a piece of toast off the plate. "Hadn't thought much about it. I've got enough in the bank that I don't need to work."

"Early retirement, huh?"

A ghost of a smile flitted over his lips. "Just over ten years too early."

So maybe a little older than I'd originally guessed, but I didn't give a shit. "I've got a proposition for you."

"I'm all ears."

"I've been working thirteen-hour days for the past two weeks because my other bartender quit."

"Shit."

"I enjoy working the bar, but I'm getting behind on paperwork and could really use someone to spare me during the slow hours right after lunch." I lifted my mug and sipped again as he studied me.

"You're offering me a bartender position?"

"If you want it, yes."

"I'm not a big talker."

"Most people would rather have an ear."

He grimaced and took a big bite of toast, chewing, gaze still latched on my eyes. "I'll do it on one condition."

"What's that?"

His blue eyes darkened as he glanced at my lips. "I stay here until I can move into my apartment."

"On the cot?" I asked with a smirk.

"No. In your bed, between your legs. Every night."

I swallowed against the sudden dryness in my throat. "You've got yourself a deal, Dominic Landon."

Nicky

I lugged all of my bins from the truck up the outside stairs to Mel's apartment, showered, and headed to Suzie's on the Harley, a new shiny key to Mel's place on my key ring. The rumble and vibrations between my legs filled me with a sense of freedom I'd never felt anywhere else. I could point the front wheel wherever the hell I wanted and ride off into the sunset.

Wouldn't mind Mel behind me, I thought while pulling up to Suzie's house.

I'd never been interested in tying myself down to an old lady, but that young woman made me think things I had no business considering. Too damn old. Too damn used up. Heaving a deep breath, I climbed off my bike and walked up the uneven cobblestone walkway to Suzie's.

I knocked and stepped back from the door.

The lock clicked, heightening my heartbeat.

She looked like shit. Straggly hair hung limply to her shoulders, the same dirty blonde as Ellen's. Dark circles lay beneath her bloodshot eyes, her gaunt cheekbones sticking out like a skull's.

I fought not to frown. "Suzie."

"Uncle Nicky." Her gaze flitted down over me, and she opened the door wide. "You might as well come on in since you don't know how to take a fucking hint to leave me the hell alone."

She shuffled away, her tattered robe hanging on bony shoulders.

I stepped into the house and caught my breath against the odor of stale cigarettes and cat piss while glancing around. I didn't remember Ellen being a pack rat hoarder, but there wasn't much room to walk around the place.

Following in Suzie's footsteps over pizza boxes, empty boxes, and containers of all sorts of shit, I struggled to control my rising anger. How the fuck had Ellen not seen what sort of environment she'd created for her only daughter? How the fuck had she not smelled the rot and mildew?

"'Scuse the mess," Suzie muttered, pushing papers off the kitchen table and slumping onto a chair.

I shoved some stuff away from the back of the other chair and sat. All sorts of crud and shit smeared across the small, round table between us. Ignoring it proved tough, but I forced myself to focus on Suzie's face.

"I'm not here to take a damn thing away from you, Suzaroo."

Tears filled her eyes, and she looked away, her jaw clenching.

"I owe you an apology. Quite a few, actually."

She turned toward me. "What for?"

"For being part of the system that provided the drugs that killed your mom. For not being here for you when you buried her. For agreeing to stay away from you the last ten years."

"Did you do it?"

"No," I lied as I'd done since ending her father's life with a single bullet between his fucking eyes.

Suzie hugged herself, shoulders slumping. "I thought for sure he would come back. I wanted him to, even though he was a mean bastard. He was my father, you know?"

I nodded.

"He never laid a hand on me like he did Mom." Tears welled again and slipped down her cheeks. "He adored me. Sang me to sleep every night. Read books to me whenever the hell I wanted him to."

Guilt hit me like a fucking knife in the gut, and I clenched my jaw.

"Why the fuck would he leave me?"

"I'm so sorry."

"I understand him not wanting to be with Mom anymore, but he loved me."

Suzie buried her head in her hands as sobs shook her thin frame.

I wanted to wrap her up in my arms, take away her pain—I'd been the bastard who'd caused it. My fucking chest ached, and my vision actually hazed for the first time since childhood.

She quieted eventually, her face pale and drawn. "I-I've got someone coming over in a couple."

Taking the hint, I stood. "Can we meet again soon? Say, for lunch or dinner—my treat?"

"Yeah." She stood, too, and motioned me back toward the front door. "Sure."

Brushed off like a fly, I realized as I pulled the door open. "I'm moving into the apartment above the drug store, but until it's open, I'm bunking in the bar's storeroom."

"Yeah, okay." She grabbed the handle as I stepped out onto the stoop and started to close me out.

"If you need anything, Suzaroo, please let me know."

"Yep. Will do."

The door clicked shut in my face.

I heaved another deep breath. *Progress. One step at a time.*

****

Mel showed me the ropes before her friend Kelly showed up at ten thirty to prep for lunch. Her friend gave us a look, brow raised, but I kept my mouth shut and actually smiled at someone other than Mel for the first time in a long fucking time.

I thought I'd felt at home in the Glider's club, but Mel's tiny apartment and bar fit me like a broken-in leather glove. I couldn't remember the last time I'd been happy, and while guilt, Suzie, and the whole fucked up situation between us overshadowed my life, the twinkling light of Mel made the hours of a day worthwhile.

It felt great having someone to tell about my short time with Suzie—minus the fact I'd killed her father and that guilt ate at my gut. Mel hugged me tightly, tears coating her eyes.

Fucking home, I thought, squeezing her in return and breathing in the subtle scent of her lavender, lemony shampoo.

The bar opened at eleven, and I stayed by Mel's side, watching and enjoying every move she made. Her swaying hips, joyful smile, and expressive whiskey-colored eyes brought out a side of me I'd never known existed—possessiveness. I hardly knew Mel, but deep inside, I felt she belonged to me. The thought didn't sit well. She was younger than Suzie, for Christ's sake, and I had nothing but a truck, Harley, and decent-sized lump sum in my bank account to call my own.

I also had no fucking plans for my future, and Mel had the whole of hers ahead of her. Falling couldn't be stopped. Neither could the sure heartache to come. She brought light and life, an addictive joy I'd never expected to find, and I had to make myself content to watch her. Soak up every second while I could until she realized she needed a younger man to fulfill whatever dreams holed up in her head.

She escaped into the office, Kelly took off for a bit after the lunch crowd dwindled, and I manned the bar.

Two older men sat a few stools away from each other, chatting it up. I left them to it and wiped spots off glasses, becoming more acquainted with country music than I wanted to.

Mel needed a new dishwasher and radio station.

Once the men left, I made my way to the office and leaned against the door jamb, arms crossed.

A smile curved Mel's full lips, but she didn't lift her attention from the paperwork on her desk. "How's it going?"

"Good. Are you getting some work done?"

"Yes, thank God." She tipped her head my way, and that damn possessive lust shot through my chest. "I really appreciate your helping me out."

"I appreciate you giving me a place to crash."

Her attention dropped to my lips, and I smirked. "I would have let you stay even if you hadn't agreed to work for me."

"Why's that?" I had no intention of prying, because I didn't really want to go there, but it seemed my mouth had issues with discretion.

"Why's that," she murmured in echo, lifting her gaze back to my eyes. "I haven't quite decided yet, but I can't seem to keep my mind off you."

I strode across her office and spun her chair around to face me. Leaning down, I placed my hands on the armrests and peered into her impassioned eyes. "I feel the same fucking way, and I don't know what to do about it."

"You could always kiss me," she said with a saucy tilt of her head and lips.

I accepted her invitation and then some, devouring her mouth, but I couldn't get enough. Dropping to my knees between her legs, I cradled her head in my hands and took complete control, groaning as she scooted closer and pressed her chest against me.

"Fuck, do I want you," I growled against her mouth.

"Shut the office door," she murmured and licked my lower lip.

I didn't need to be told twice.

Mel crooked a finger when I turned from locking the door.

I had every intention of bending her over the desk, but as I drew near, she grabbed my belt buckle and yanked me close. "I want your cock in my mouth."

"Fuck, yes."

Her fingers shook while trying to undo the buckle, but I held still, allowing her to take what she wanted. She reached into my leathers and pulled my cock free. Her tongue swiped over her lower lip as she leaned forward.

"Goddamn," I groaned as her lips closed around me. Threading my fingers through her long locks, I held on for dear fucking life as she bottomed out against my base, my cock down her throat. "Do you like having my cock in your mouth?"

I cursed again as she swallowed and backed off, cheeks hollowed, the hot suction of her mouth taking me to the edge so damn quick I felt like a teenager again.

Mel dug her fingers into my ass and took me deep again, right down her fucking throat.

"You're going to make me blow in a matter of seconds," I said, my voice tight as my balls.

She backed off and smiled, looking up at me through her lashes. "Blow away," she mumbled around my mushroom head.

"Fuck." I held her head and thrust, shoving my cock into her wet mouth, her tongue lathing, coaxing the ache in my balls to release. "I'm going to shoot my cum down your throat, and you're going to swallow every drop I give you."

She moaned around me, and I gave over to the need to come, bucking my hips, loving every scrape of her teeth and swirl of her tongue.

My balls seized, and I slammed down her throat a handful of times until cum shot up through my cock. She swallowed, sucking down every drop just like I'd told her to do.

Knees going weak and sucking wind, I pulled her mouth off me and yanked her up into my arms. I kissed her hard, not giving two shits that remnants of my cum coated her lips.

Fucking mine, and that's all there is to it.
****

I could taste the sexual tension between us all damn night. We worked the bar together from about five o'clock on, and every brush of her fingertips, heated glance, and suggestive smile raced need through me. Being buried balls deep in her soaked, tight pussy was all I could think about.

Silent curses rang in my head damn near all night long, and until she finally locked the front door, I wanted to fuck her against the nearest wall.

Restraint, I told myself, thinking about how I wanted her sprawled out on her bed, thighs wide, pink pussy glistening.

She flicked the lights and sauntered toward me through the dim light from the streetlight a ways down the road. "Fuck here or upstairs?" she asked, running her palms up over my chest.

I grabbed her hand and turned toward the office without a word. Anticipation sped through me worse than the night I'd lost my virginity at fourteen.

I ripped off my shirt and kicked off my boots the

second we walked through the apartment door. Into the bedroom, lights flicked on, and I turned Mel into my arms. "I want you naked and on the bed. You've got five seconds, or I'm going to tear these clothes off you."

"Promise?"

"Four..." I pushed off my leathers and stood naked before I reached one.

She'd pulled her shirt off, revealing a black lacy bra, and got as far as shimmying her tight jeans and panties to her ankles before I picked her up and tossed her onto the bed. Her smirk egging me on, I yanked off her boots and jeans.

I leaned over her body, my breath against her ear. "Bend over the edge of the bed. Ass in the air."

Her breath caught, her wide eyes locked on my face as I backed away.

"Now, little girl."

She scooted to the edge of the bed and flipped over, showing off her gorgeous ass.

I rubbed a hand over one rounded cheek as her feet settled on the floor, my heart thumping in my chest. "You've been teasing me all damn day."

"Mmm."

"I think a little punishment is in order." I swung, my palm slapping on the side of her ass I'd been caressing.

Mel jolted and squeaked.

"Too much?"

"No." She breathed the word like a fucking horny-as-hell siren.

I spanked her again.

She wiggled her ass at me as my handprints rose in red across her pale globes.

"Little minx." I let loose with a half-dozen unrestrained swats, pleased to see her lower lip between her teeth, tears leaking from the corners of her eyes. "On your back," I said, my voice rasping with the need coursing through my blood.

Studying my face, she obeyed like a good little girl, wincing while scooting her backside across the sheets.

"I'm going to lick every inch of this sweet pussy," I said, crawling between her legs and wrapping my arms around her thighs and holding her tight.

"Yes," she whispered, trying to lift her pussy toward my face.

Breathing deep filled my lungs with her tangy scent, and my mouth flooded with drool. "I'm going to eat you out until you come all over my tongue."

Mel tried to lift her hips again with a moan, and I ran my tongue from her asshole to her clit.

"You taste so fucking good." I repeated the action, pausing to circle the hole of her pussy, lapping at the moisture dripping from her. "So wet…"

"All your fault," she said with a gasp as I flicked her clit with the tip of my tongue.

I pressed a finger deep into her tight channel, rubbing the pad of my finger lightly over her g-spot. "I do this to you, little girl. I make you this way."

"God, yes." She arched her back and wiggled her hips.

Grinning, I removed my finger from her sopping pussy and ate her out like I'd promised—every inch, exploring every valley and hole, licking, nibbling, and sucking on her flesh until she bucked beneath me.

"I'm going to come!"

"Give it to me." I plunged my tongue into her tight pussy and rubbed her clit between two fingers.

She grasped my head, and her thighs held me captive in their tight grip. "God! Nicky!"

A rush of moisture swept over my tongue and dripped off my chin. I growled against the throb in my balls and thrust my aching cock into the mattress while lapping up every trace of her cum.

"Please..." She writhed beneath my hold, and I finally tore my attention from her swollen folds, kissing my way up over her pubic bone to her belly button. "I need you. Please."

She stared up at me with those damn whiskey-kissed eyes, and a fucking sledgehammer-like blow knocked the breath from me.

Too horny to think too much on the feeling, I grabbed a condom from the bed stand where I'd thrown them the night before and sheathed myself in record time. The second I settled between her thighs again, she wrapped her legs around me and pulled me close.

Although I wanted to slam into the hilt with one vicious thrust, I slid in slow and easy, giving her time to adjust to my girth in case she was sore from the night before.

"Oh my God." She arched her back, pressing her breasts against me, and I licked my way up her exposed neck while rocking into her tight heat. "So damn good," she breathed, her heels digging into my ass and hands clasping my back.

I nibbled her jaw bone to her ear and sucked her lobe between my teeth, her pussy clamping and releasing with every slow thrust of my hips. In and out, gentle glides of pure friction. The thought of having her without a condom between us rose to mind, and I decided I'd have her bare, her juices coating my cock, my cum shooting deep inside of her.

My balls tightened, and I growled my appreciation of the thought into her neck while thrusting a little harder.

"Yes." Her nails dug into the muscles lining my spine.

I angled my hips and ground my pelvis against her clit with every deep thrust.

Mel moaned beneath me, and rather than hold her still, I planked on my elbows and gave her freedom to move. She lifted her hips to meet me, but I couldn't go deep enough. I wanted inside of her head. Her heart.

"Look at me."

Her long lashes fluttered open, and I felt myself drowning in the passion pouring from her gorgeous eyes.

We stared at each other, her lips parted with each panted breath. Everything disappeared from my mind but Mel and her hold on my body, every upward thrust of her hips as I slid into her pussy over and over again.

My chest ached like a motherfucker but in the best way possible. At a loss for words, I lowered myself against her sweat-dampened body and kissed her with every bit of passion coursing through me. Buried myself balls deep inside of her again and again.

She tore her lips from mine, panting for breath. "I'm going to come."

I worked my arm beneath her ass and angled my hips to take her deeper. "Take me with you," I said, grinding my pelvis against her clit.

"Oh fuck!" She shrieked, her pussy clamping around me.

My balls fucking exploded, and I hollered her name, slamming into her with erratic thrusts as spurt after spurt of cum shot into the condom while she continued to spasm around my length.

"Shit," I growled on the last thrust and collapsed on top of her.

A shudder rippled down through her body, and my cock jerked as she squeezed her inner muscles. She went limp beneath me, her arms falling from my back, heels slipping down the backs of my thighs.

"Good and truly wrecked," she whispered, a smile in her voice.

Face buried in her neck, I couldn't help but think the same thing.

Mel

Nicky and I fell into a comfortable pattern a hell of a lot quicker than I expected. Morning sex, coffee, and toast, then down to the bar to clean up from the night before since we'd been too anxious to get to bed once I locked up.

We worked well alongside each other behind the bar, and the locals quickly seemed to accept him as a permanent fixture by the end of the week.

I wanted more, though. Working thirteen hours a day every day had been all fine and well until Nicky came along. We'd managed to grab a couple of short rides on his Harley, and each and every one had me ready to ride his cock the second we got back to the apartment.

Work always called, though.

When I put a help wanted sign in the window, Nicky didn't question me. Neither did Kelly. While she still shot eye rolls my way, she told me after a week of seeing how Nicky watched me that she approved. I wouldn't have given a shit if she hadn't, though.

Nicky was it for me. Don't know how the hell I knew it or even when the truth solidified in my brain, but he belonged to me. I belonged to him, too, but he didn't know it yet.

Suzi came in and had lunch with him once after he begged—or so he claimed. She looked a mess. Run down and drugged out. Sick as hell.

If she didn't get help, I feared she'd end up like her mom, and while it wasn't my business, I couldn't keep my mouth shut.

Curled up and facing Nicky, our heads sharing a pillow, I decided to hell with it. "We need to get Suzie some help."

"I've told her twice I would pay for rehab."

My brow rose. "What'd she say?"

"No, both times, even though I've told her she's going to end up like her mother."

"What did she think about your ideas for fixing up her house?"

"She complained about money and brushed off my offer to pay."

He'd told me a couple days earlier that he planned to offer to paint the exterior, fix up the yard, and re-do the entire interior—once all of Ellen's junk found its way into dumpsters. After hearing him explain the squalor Suzie lived in, my heart had melted at his desire to help her.

"Saw Sheriff Elliott talking your ear off earlier tonight," I said. "Is he still hounding you to help him?"

"Yes." Nicky heaved a slow breath. "Sometimes the guilt over my old life hits me like a shitload of bricks, and I'm tempted to spill my guts."

"Why don't you?" I asked, running my hand over his bearded jaw, the soft whiskers tickling my palm.

"If the Gliders ever found out I let the law in on brotherhood secrets, I'd be force-fed enough lead to open a bullet factory."

A shiver slid along my spine. Unsure what to say, I leaned in and pressed my lips lightly to his.

He wrapped his arm around me and pulled me closer, our bodies touching from chest to toes. His warmth seeped through my skin, and I wanted to bury myself inside of him, latch on forever.

"Sometimes I feel like I can't get close enough." I heard myself say the thought I'd had more than once.

"Yes." He kissed me again, his soft, full lips and sweet breath sending shivers over my bare skin. "I can't get enough of you, Mel."

I pulled my head back so I could see his sated blue eyes in the light of the lamp I'd left on. "I can't get enough of you either."

"That's a good thing, right?"

The first hint of insecurity I'd heard or seen from him. Big, brawny man with a dominant nature wondering about us with uncertainty.

I smiled. "It's a great thing."

His slow smile warmed me through. "When's the new girl start?"

"Tomorrow."

"Think she'll be okay to take an afternoon shift alone later this week?"

"Should be. Why?"

"A day of freedom. I want you on the back of my Harley, and we're going across the Kancamagus Highway."

"God, I haven't been over there for years. Can we stop at the waterfalls and dip our toes in?"

He squeezed me tight. "We can stop wherever the hell you want. I just want you on my bike with the wind whipping around us."

I snuggled against him like I'd done every night since that first night he came to my bed. Breathing in his subtle cologne and the scent of pure male, I realized I'd gone from being wrecked to being in love. Would he believe me if I told him after so short a time, though?

"Too fast, too old," Mom had said after having us over for breakfast the day before, but she knew I would do whatever the hell I wanted. "Just be careful," she'd whispered as I hugged her goodbye.

I knew what she'd meant. My father had stopped in town and hung around long enough to get what he wanted from my mom before jetting off to God knows where.

"Men don't buy the cow if they get to milk it for free," she'd continued on in my ear.

I had rolled my eyes and peeled myself out of her arms. "Gotta go open up the bar, Mom."

She'd let me go, fluttering her fingers at Nicky.

"What are you thinking about?" Nicky asked, drawing me back to the present.

"My mom thinks you're too old for me," I blurted.

"I am."

"Bullshit." I snuggled in closer. "Age doesn't matter."

"It does if you plan on settling down someday and having children."

I snorted. "If I ever say I want to have kids, shoot me."

His sudden chuckle rumbled in his chest squished against my face.

"What's so funny?"

"I've never heard someone your age sound so adamant about not having kids."

"God." I shuddered while memories of the toddler time at the library came to mind. "I used to help my mom out in the children's library. No. Thank. You."

He laughed again, and I soaked in the rare sound. Once he quieted, he ran his fingers through my hair. "You might change your mind someday."

That hint of insecurity laced his low voice again, and I pulled back to look him full in the face. "As God as my witness, I never have, nor shall I ever want children of my own." I popped an eyebrow up. "Clear enough?"

His eyes twinkled in the dim light. "Crystal."

"Good. Now that's settled, kiss me again."

He groaned but obeyed. "You're going to be the

death of me," he murmured not for the first time against my lips, and I smiled.

****

Four days later found me on the back of Nicky's Harley, new leather pants and jacket hugging my curves. He'd gone to the Harley shop in Conway the day before and brought home gifts.

The apartment was cramped as it was with all of his bins stuffed here and there. He hadn't mentioned his place above the drug store, but it was supposed to be available the following week.

I didn't want him to leave. The thought of being alone again every night pinged my chest in a very unpleasant, shitty way. Sure, we'd hinted at a future, but we had yet to discuss anything.

The wind whipped around us, just like Nicky had promised, and I closed my eyes, breathing in the scents of spring, woods, and fresh air. Harley rumbling beneath us, we slowly made our way up the Kancamagus Highway, stopping at every pull off to cut the engine and enjoy the views.

I'd packed some sandwiches, so once we hit the crest of the mountains, we pulled into the overlook and enjoyed a picnic in the grass.

"Best day ever," I said, once full and lying on my back to soak up some spring rays of sun shining down on us. "I forgot what it was like to have freedom." Nicky lounged on his side facing me, and I turned my head. "Thank you for this."

Badass tatts covered his muscular arms, but gentleness poured from his small smile. "Thank you for sharing the day with me."

We stared at each other in comfortable silence as we often did, my mind enjoying a daydream in la la land where happily-ever-afters existed and true love conquered all.

"What are you thinking?" I asked, having to know what darkened the blue shade of his eyes.

"I'm thinking that I want you."

Arousal sprang to life between my thighs, and I smiled. "You seem to think that a lot."

"Yes, but I'm thinking about having you bare. No condom, nothing between us."

"I've never been with someone like that."

"Ever?"

I shook my head.

"Are you on birth control?" he asked.

"Yes. I'm clean, too."

"So am I."

My smile widened at the idea of his cock sliding into me unsheathed, skin on skin. "Want to take a little walk in the woods? Get lost for an hour or two?"

Nicky's lips twitched as one eyebrow raised.

My cell vibrated in my back pocket.

"Shit." I rolled and pulled it out, hoping the new girl wasn't having any trouble.

Kelly's name showed up onscreen.

"Everything okay?" I asked, sitting up.

"No." She sounded panicked. "Is Nicky right there?"

My heart thumped heavy in my chest. "Yes. What's wrong?"

"I need to talk to him."

Frowning, I handed the phone to Nicky. "It's Kelly."

He sat up and took the phone. "Hey, Kelly." His brow furrowed. Eyes closed. "Fuck." He rubbed a hand down over his face and nodded. "Yeah, I do. I'll head straight there." He offered me the phone with a harsh "Fuck!" and hopped to his feet.

"Kelly," I said while standing, my attention on Nicky as he strode away.

"His niece overdosed."

"Shit."

"She's alive, but that's all I know."

"Shit," I said again, grabbing our picnic stuff and scrambling after Nicky as he made for the Harley. "Can you shut down the bar after dinner for me?"

"Sure thing. Hope everything is okay."

I muttered an agreement and hit the "end" button.

Seconds later, the Harley roared to life, and I held on tight as Nicky tore off back the way we'd come.

I couldn't begin to imagine what ran through his head as we sped back down the highway. Arms wrapped around his waist and cheek pressed against his back, I tried to send him all of my positive energy. Like an immovable rock, he focused on the road.

Nicky pulled off the highway into town, and I sat up straight, my heart falling. I'd expected him to head straight to the hospital, where I could be by his side and support him. He stopped in front of the bar, feet down on the ground on either side of the bike, engine still running.

A heaviness settled over me and tears pricked my eyes, but I took the hint and climbed off, grabbing our picnic stuff from the saddlebags. "I hope everything is okay," I said, catching his gaze. "Good luck."

Eyes shuttered and lips pursed, he nodded once and took off again, leaving me alone.

The early birds had shown up for dinner, I noted through the front windows. Old Toothless and Mrs. Hanks both peered through the glass at me. Forcing a smile, I went in and greeted everyone by name before disappearing into the office. I dropped my stuff on the desk and flopped into the chair.

Kelly swept in, eyes wide and full of concern.

"Guess he doesn't want me with him," I said at the obvious question etched on her face.

My hurt must have shown, because she came over and hugged me. "God, I hope she's okay."

"Me, too." My throat ached, but I refused to cry. Nicky faced heartache from almost losing his last family member as he had his sister. "I can't imagine how he's feeling right now. Dammit." I swiped an escaped tear from my cheek as Kelly backed away.

"You really care about him, don't you?"

"Yes." I pulled my phone from my pocket and put it on the desk. It would be another half hour or so until he got to the hospital. I hoped he would call with an update quickly.

Nicky

I reverted to my old ways and broke every law getting to the hospital. My mind raced as fast as my Harley, but numbness grasped my body, and the second I caught sight of Suzie in the hospital bed, the world crashed in on me. I clenched my jaw against the sudden tightness in my throat.

Ashen, gaunt face, pale lips parted ... she lay unmoving, eyes closed. Lank hair lay under her head. Her hand was hooked up to an IV, and tubes and wires stretched all over the place. I hesitated to approach, not sure where to sit or what part of her I could touch.

I stood and stared, relief Suzie lived and anger over the drugs wasting her life warring for first spot in my head. My eyes burned and hands itched to squeeze the life out of her dealer—whoever the fucker was. Never mind the fact the Gliders were probably his supplier.

A lavender, lemony scent similar to Mel's shampoo slipped past my nose, and longing for her slammed into me like a fucking cement truck barreling through the other emotions clogging my brain.

I should have brought her with me, I realized, slumping onto the chair beside Suzie. Her presence alone would have offered comfort and calmed me the fuck down. Her inner joy—even in the time ahead I faced—would have given me something to hold on to so I wouldn't lose my fucking mind in its war.

I scrubbed a hand over my face and along my beard while heaving a breath.

Mel had responsibilities, a business she couldn't just up and leave because my niece made a stupid-ass choice.

Did she do it intentionally?

"Dammit, Suzaroo." I picked up her hand and clasped it between mine. Cold and clammy. She didn't respond. "The fuck were you thinking?"

She missed Ellen—more than I did. Losing the only person you have is tough enough to face sober, let alone as an addict. Had she felt she had nothing to live for? No sense of purpose? Or was she just trying to escape the sorrow, the pain of a broken heart?

Sitting in the beep-filled, bleach-scented room, I considered the lives lost to me. Grandparents and parents, my only sister, and a couple of old brothers from the Gliders I used to kill for. The only ones I should have defended in such a way had been taken from me—all except one.

Suzie let out a sigh, and her eyelids fluttered open.

"Suzaroo." Throat still tight, I somehow managed a smile.

Her gaze landed on me, her eyes glassy. She blinked twice and licked her lips. "I'm either alive or in hell," she said, her voice raspy and slurred, "'cuz God knows you'll never get into heaven."

My huff of laughter lightened the load on my shoulders enough I felt I could breathe again.

"The fuck happened?" she asked, glancing around the curtained area and blinking slowly.

I squeezed her hand. "You overdosed."

"Oh, fuck." She closed her eyes again, and a tear slipped down her cheek.

I wanted to ask if she'd meant to do it, but bit my tongue, allowing her to wake up a little more.

"Am I okay?" she asked a few minutes later, eyes still shut, words still slurred.

"Yes."

"Thank God."

Accidental. The rest of the weight fell off my shoulders, and I heaved a huge breath.

"Sorry, Uncle."

A sob ripped from her, and I leaned over, hugging her frail body the best I could. "It's gonna be all right, Suzaroo," I whispered. "I'm going to get you the best care. Get you clean. I promise I'll do whatever you need to get healthy again."

Suzie continued to cry, and I only sat back when a nurse pushed past the curtain.

"You're awake," the nurse said with a smile. "How are you doing, Suzanne?"

"It's Suzie, and I feel like shit," my niece muttered as she slow-blinked again.

The nurse checked vitals while asking a few more questions and making notes on Suzie's chart.

"We're going to get you upstairs in a room soon, okay?" the nurse said, her hand on Suzie's shoulder.

"'K."

The nurse scurried away on squeaky shoes.

"I didn't mean to do it," Suzie said, her shaky hand reaching for me.

I leaned forward and folded her bony hand in mine.

"I-I got some drugs from a new guy. The second I injected it, I knew something wasn't right."

My gut twisted. "Who was the guy?"

"Goes by Pauly ... Delgado, I think." Suzie sighed and closed her eyes again. "Lives in Rochester near my dealer. Since Mikey Mac was out of town, he hooked me up."

"Mikey's your usual dealer?"

"Yeah."

"Mikey's last name is Mac?"

Suzie cracked her eyelids open and peered at me with hazed-over, watery eyes. "Why you asking?"

Because I want to put a bullet through his fucking brain. "Just curious. Is that who your mom got her drugs through, too?"

"Yeah. Mac stands for MacDonald or MacDougal … something like that. Can't remember. We went to high school together."

I made some mental notes while she chatted, her words starting to bleed into one another after yawning a dozen or so times.

"Why don't you sleep for a while," I said, patting her hand. "I'll be here all night and make sure you're taken care of."

"Thanks, Uncle."

"You're getting a second chance to start over, Suzaroo. You don't know how happy that makes me."

A small smile lifted her pale lips as her eyes rolled back into her head. "We're both getting a new beginning, aren't we?" she murmured.

Her question echoed in my head long after I found a quiet, private spot and pulled out my cell phone. While I wanted to put a bullet through Mikey Mac and Pauly Delgado's skulls, I'd left that kind of life behind forever.

Trusting the law to deal with the two men wouldn't come easy, but I could at least ensure the two men found their asses in jail before Suzie made her way through rehab.

Passing on the names to Sheriff Elliott was the best I could do. The rest would be up to the cops.

If, however, either fucker got away with their crimes and came anywhere near Suzie again, ending their shit-lives would come damn easy. Hell, I wished they'd come sniffing around hoping for a sale, just so I could see justice served for myself.

Mel

I finally crawled into bed at one—without having heard from Nicky. I had locked up and scrubbed down the bar, my stomach in knots. The not knowing, the being out of his life when I could have helped, hurt like a bitch. Showed me exactly how much I meant to him beyond a freebie place to crash and a pussy or ass to fuck whenever the mood struck.

My ears strained for the rumble of his bike. The creak of the exterior stairs leading to my apartment. Every passing car roused me from the shitty sleep I managed to grasp.

A chill swept through me while I lay in my bed, the sheets beside me cold when they should be wrapped around the best thing to ever happen to me. If only he felt the same.

I gave up at six and crawled from bed. Slumped in uncomfortable silence at my kitchen table, I sucked down two cups of coffee, wishing for a shot or two of something a little stronger to go with it.

The temptation to call the hospital came on strong, but Suzie wasn't my family. The chance of me getting any info was close to none. I considered asking for her room, but if Nicky had wanted me there or wished to talk to me, he'd have called.

Kelly texted me at eight asking how Suzie was. Replying that I didn't know sucked ass.

I hopped in the shower, my aching chest to the hot spray while scrubbing my hair. A few tears mixed in with the water droplets on my face as longing for Nicky rolled over me again.

How had I become so wrapped up in him so quickly? Imagining the next day—the next year—

without him in my bed, behind the bar with me, had me praying to a god I didn't believe in. My stomach churned, and no amount of swallowing eased the pain in the back of my throat.

The bathroom door squeaked open, and I paused in squirting conditioner into my hand to peer through the fogged shower door.

Nicky.

My knees weakened as sudden lightness filled my heart.

He tugged his shirt off overhead, drying out my mouth, and when he pushed down his leather pants, my breath caught in my throat. My mind raced over the need for answers—what he felt, if he wanted more than just the physical with me—but the dark circles lining his bleak eyes kept my mouth shut.

Stomach fluttering, I put the conditioner bottle back down and wiped water from my face as he stepped into the shower with me.

"Suzie?" I whispered.

"Gonna be okay." He crowded against me, wrapping his arms around my waist.

I melted into him and he took my mouth with a ferocity I matched, pouring out my hurt and frustration with every swipe of my tongue and nip of my teeth.

His cock swelled, pressing against my belly, and I moaned while rubbing myself against him.

Nicky grasped my ass and lifted me like I weighed nothing, holding me tight against him.

I wrapped my legs around his waist, locking my ankles.

"I need you," he groaned, sliding his cock along my pussy lips.

"Yes," I said and captured his mouth again, uncaring that in the moment he only needed me in a physical sense.

He lined up and thrust in with no resistance—skin on skin. I groaned into his mouth as his arms tightened around me, holding me in a vise grip.

I'd never had a man without a condom before. Exquisite torture—knowing nothing separated us and that Nicky was inside of me as deep as he could get flooded me with unexplainable emotion. My heart hammered in my chest and tears pricked my eyes, but not from hurt or sadness.

I tried to wiggle, and he began to move his hips, holding my ass with one hand, the other around my waist.

Fingers in his hair and legs squeezing, I took all he gave, my climax rising to the surface faster than I thought possible. His strength, raw power, and hard muscles filled me with lust, soaked my pussy around his thrusting cock.

I panted for breath against his mouth, and he pulled his head back. Blue eyes, lust-hazed beyond the exhaustion, peered at me. Water drops clung to his long lashes and beard.

"I need you to come around my cock, Mel. I need you to make me forget all the fucking shit in my brain."

My body obeyed, my climax sweeping around from my toes and shattering over me. I cried out his name while convulsing in his arms.

He bit my collarbone, muffling his shout, and his cum shot hot, deep inside of me. Every spurt sent a wave of euphoria over me, and I clung to his wet skin, anchoring myself to reality.

Eyes closed, I soaked in the tingles racing through me as he calmed, still buried inside of me. He rained kisses on my neck and jaw, eventually taking my mouth in a gentle kiss.

I slid my legs down, and he backed away, leaving me empty, our combined cum dripping between my thighs. Shoulder slumped, he stood like a defeated man.

"Here." I turned him into the spray, grabbed the soap, and began washing him.

Head tilted back into the water, arms at his side, he slouched and allowed me to attend to him. His cock stirred in my soapy hands, but I continued down his thighs and turned him to work my way up his backside.

I washed him, caring for him the best way I could, even though he didn't want me emotionally or mentally.

"Do you want coffee?" I asked while putting the soap back in the dish, a slight tremor in my voice.

"Just a bed." His low voice rasped, probably from being up all night.

I climbed out of the shower and grabbed an extra towel, fighting off the tears stinging my eyelids and the desire to discuss what was going on between us. Nicky was obviously in no state to have a serious conversation, let alone deal with a woman's tears.

Without a word, we dried off, and I tucked my towel around my chest while Nicky hung his on the hook on the back of the bathroom door. Naked, he staggered across my bedroom, pulled back the blankets, and collapsed like a drunk man.

I pulled the covers up over him, and he rubbed his face against my pillow, breathing deeply. That sweet ache swept through me but didn't bring a smile to my face as it usually did. I grabbed some clothes, shut off the light, and left him to sleep, wishing my mind would shut off as easily.

Nicky

The subtle scent of Mel's lavender, lemony shampoo surrounded me, and I hugged her closer, my cock swelling.

Damn pillow, I grumbled to myself as the fluffy down squished against my chest. I cracked an eyelid open to find the clock reading almost two thirty.

I'd spent the night in the ER by Suzie's side, my heart torn. Suzie had been in and out, half-asleep and groggy as hell. As her next of kin, I'd taken charge and lined up the best care available for her, including a nice long stay at a nearby rehab clinic once she detoxed.

Thankful didn't begin to explain how I felt over the fact the drugs Suzie shot up hadn't taken her life. Losing my sister and my niece within a few weeks of each other from the same fucking drugs my old brothers dealt would have done me in.

I should have asked Mel to go to the hospital with me, I thought again while squeezing her pillow and breathing her in. I had missed her every second while sitting on that damn hard-backed chair, beeps and murmurings of others in the ER filling my ears.

She wouldn't want to deal with my personal shit, though.

Rolling onto my back, I released Mel's pillow and stretched. I considered getting out of bed and showering, but I couldn't bring myself to move from the soft, sweet-smelling mattress beneath me.

The door leading down to the bar squeaked open, and I listened as Mel moved around the kitchen. Brewing coffee, I noted with appreciation as the scent filtered into the bedroom a few minutes later.

She peeked her head in the cracked-open

doorway. "You're awake."

I motioned her over. "Somewhat."

The mattress beside me dipped as she sat, her shuttered eyes and body language telling me something was on her mind.

I lifted a hand to brush long strands of her hair over her shoulder. "What's wrong?"

She shrugged. "I don't want to bother you with my emotional shit when you've got so much going on."

"Emotional shit, huh?"

With a nod, she glanced away.

Gaze narrowed, I captured her around the waist and pulled her down on top of me. "I missed you yesterday," I said against the shell of her ear.

"You did?" Her voice caught as I sucked her lobe between my lips.

"I wanted you with me, but figured you couldn't be stuck at the hospital all night with me."

Mel pulled back and peered down at me, tears coating her eyes. "I thought you didn't want me there."

"Well, I did."

"I told Kelly to shut down after the dinner rush slowed when she'd called us on top of the mountain."

"I didn't hear you tell her that, or I would have gone straight to the hospital."

Her small smile flooded me with happiness, and she lay down on my chest again with a sigh.

I held her close, my lips against her hair. "Suzie's going to go through a detox program, then I'm shipping her off to rehab. I want you to go with me when I take her."

"How do you think Suzie will feel about that?"

"I don't give a shit. If I'm in her life—and I am—then so are you. Besides, I'm paying for it."

"You're a good man, Dominic Landon."

I snorted. "Hardly."

Mel nuzzled her face against my chest, her lips trailing wet kisses in a senseless pattern and hardening my cock between the warmth of her thighs.

"Is the new girl on the clock?"

She lifted her head and ran her thumb over my lower lip. "Yes."

"Take off your jeans," I said, lifting her off me and pushing the sheet covering me past my waist. My cock sprang up, drawing her attention. I palmed myself, slowly jerking while she scurried to get every stitch of her clothing off.

She started to climb on the bed, but I grabbed her hips. "Sit on my face. I want to taste your sweet pussy."

Pupils huge, she bit on the inside of her lip and crawled over me.

Settling her thighs on either side of my head put her wet pussy directly above me, and I yanked her down onto my face, shoving my tongue deep into her. With a moan, she wiggled her hips, and I ate her out like a starving man, lapping, burying my nose in her tangy sweetness, nibbling and sucking until she panted.

"Now ride me, little girl," I growled, pushing her down over my chest. "Take what you need."

Mel slid the rest of the way down my body, leaving a smear of her arousal across my skin. Her pussy lips slickened down over my cock, and the second she lined up with the throbbing head, I shoved in with one thrust.

A shudder rippled through both of us, and Mel bit down on her lower lip as I pushed her up to sit on me. My hands full of her breasts, I rolled her nipples and held still as she gyrated her hips.

Emotion flooded over her face, pupils dominating the whiskey color of her eyes. A small smile lifted her lips as she began rocking along my length, her wetness coating my pelvis.

"You love my hard cock, don't you?" I asked, pinching her nipples. "Shoved all up that tight little pussy of yours."

She gasped. "God, yes."

I thrust as she took me deep, drawing another gasp from her. "You're the only one I want riding me. Ever." She leaned down over me, and I grabbed her hips, holding her still as my balls tightened to the point of pain. "I love you, Mel," I whispered, my attention locked on her face.

Tears filled her eyes again. "I love you, too, Nicky. So damn much it hurts."

And I thought happiness had found me before. Fucking unbridled joy rolled over me, and I leaned up to capture her mouth, taking control. I pumped in and out of her soaked pussy, her moans spurring me on faster.

"I'm going to fill you with my cum so you'll never forget you're mine," I said, so fucking close stars darted my vision.

"Yes!" Mel arched her back, thrusting her breasts at me as her pussy clamped down on my length.

With a shout, I gave over and fucked her with everything I had, my balls exploding spurt after spurt deep inside of her tightness.

Arms clenched around her, I held on as her pussy milked every drop from me and we stilled, chests heaving for air.

Strands of her hair clung to my damp face, and I closed my eyes, soaking in the happiness she'd brought to my life. "You're it for me, Mel." I squeezed her tight. "If I can't have you in my life, if you aren't my future, then I might as well curl up and die because that's where I was headed before I found you."

A sigh whispered past her lips against my ear. "I knew you belonged to me the second I laid eyes on you," she said.

I fucking grinned like a fool. "Does that mean I get to keep the apartment key you gave me?"

Mel lifted her head and touched her fingertips to my smiling lips. "Yes."

I flicked my tongue along the pad of her middle finger. "You're mine forever, Mel."

"Yes," she whispered again, filling up every piece of my soul with her light.

The End

DEDICATION

For the men who dedicate their lives to loving their women, baggage and all.

FALLEN GLIDERS MC: VOLUME ONE

Fallen Gliders MC, 2

Lynn Burke

Copyright © 2018

Hawk

I sat on a barstool waiting for my drink, toothpick between my teeth, my Fallen Gliders brothers' voices and the bar's din a buzz in my brain. Bikers and women meandered by the picture window I sat in front of, but no one of interest snagged my attention.

Sturgis drew all sorts—one percenters like us, motorcycle clubs, and rider clubs, but my favorite were the wild women looking for a cock to fill their cunt—or ass. At least, that's what I used to enjoy about Sturgis.

Getting pussy had always come easy for me as a teenager, but the day I earned my colors and put the FG logo on my back, I no longer had to go looking for it. The club whores were always up for a hard fuck, but as the years passed, I'd grown bored with their fake-ass moans and gaping holes. Even Jonny, our president and my best friend waiting to down a whiskey beside me, agreed we needed new blood in the club.

We'd been in Sturgis for almost a week, and I

hadn't fucked a single woman. My outlook on life sucked the previous couple of months, to the point the thought of having my cock shoved down a willing throat or burying myself balls-deep in some random cunt didn't even twitch my dick. I felt like a windblown leaf with no sense of purpose, no desire for sex or companionship. I'd taken to drinking harder stuff than my usual beer but knew the slump I floundered in wouldn't end well unless I decided to pick my ass up and figure out my life.

Perhaps today's the day, I told myself, picking up the shot of whiskey our waitress sat in front of me.

A flash of red-brown hair drew my gaze to the far left before I could pop out the toothpick and down my drink. A little butterfly with gray-green eyes flashing along with her wide smile. Dimple, full lips, high cheekbones—a fucking model in a tight tank and Daisy Dukes.

My cock thickened inside my leather pants, and my head turned as she slowly passed by the picture window, her face animated and lips moving as she chatted with her friends, the joyful gleam in her eyes snaring me tight. She radiated life, an exuberant, light step while I wallowed in my shit life.

Jealousy and yearning for what she experienced clenched my chest, and I found myself rubbing a hand over tattooed pecs I spent hours sculpting on a daily basis.

The little butterfly passed beyond the window, and I sat back, not realizing I'd leaned forward to keep her in sight.

"Finally see something worth fucking?" Jonny asked with an elbow to my ribs.

"Fuck, yeah. Reddish hair—not the dyed kind—and tits out to here," I said around my toothpick, holding my hand out a few inches away from my chest. "Young and full of life."

One of Jonny's eyebrows rose. "What the fuck you sitting here for?"

I hesitated to glance around the group of men—fellow Fallen Gliders from across the States, discussing the lighter aspect of business. A large meeting had taken place the night before, the heads of the chapters sitting down to discuss the future of our club. Just more depressing shit to pile on life.

"Go on," Jonny encouraged, elbowing me again.

I hopped off my stool and pushed my way through the crowd for the front door. At six-foot-five, I had no trouble seeing over most of the heads bobbing to my right as I stepped out onto the sidewalk.

The roar of mufflers and cranking music from Christ knew where filled my ears as I breathed in the scents of exhaust, sweat, and cheap perfume in the night air. I took a half-dozen steps to the right, scanning the crowd of people on the sidewalk in front of me before pulling up short. No fucking way I was going to find her unless I acted like an asshole and shoved people out of my way while hurrying the way she'd gone.

Curses flew from my lips while I turned back toward the bar. A voice in my head sang a country hit, reminding me that if we were meant to be, it'd be.

"No fucking luck?" Jonny asked as I slumped back onto the stool.

My scowl sufficed for an answer.

Tipping back my head for the whiskey burn didn't help my shit mood. Neither did the bloody burger and pile of fries fifteen minutes later. Thoughts of the little butterfly warred with depression in my mind, and I called it an early night, leaving my brothers behind. The quietness of the hotel didn't offer anything but a hot shower where I could blow the load that had been building in my balls for weeks.

At least I had a semi-purpose ... find the vivacious little butterfly and steal some of her joy in life for myself.

For the next two days, the memory of the mystery woman's eyes haunted me, causing my dick to stay in a perpetual state of stiffness. Jerking off only gained me an hour or two of relief, before the need for a real pussy swelled me to the point of pain again. My fucking balls ached with the need to explode into a tight cunt until my cum leaked out of the abused hole. It fucking sucked that the thought of anyone but the fluttering little butterfly didn't do jack shit for me.

In those two days, I could have easily pounded into a handful of willing women, but I wanted more. I wanted the woman with life flashing in her eyes. I wanted those pert tits of hers wrapped around my cock as I shot my spunk up over her face.

Jonny and I along with a few others from our club rumbled into town mid-morning and found places to park. We'd seen all the bikes, clasped countless hands and shoulders, and taken in more than an eyeful of painted bodies with nothing more than tassels or stickers covering the owners' nipples since arriving in Sturgis ten days earlier.

No fucking shame, those women.

I used to love it.

I climbed off my bike and led the way into the bar we'd agreed on for lunch. Since I considered myself Jonny's secret service agent, my head swiveled as I took in the people around me, eyes and ears alert for any bullshit. As I'd reached the open door, I cast one last look down the sidewalk to my left.

The little butterfly and her two friends crossed the road, laughing with a lighthearted carelessness that clenched my chest again.

I pulled up short.

"The fuck?" Jonny cursed as he bumped into me.

"It's her," I muttered and lit out after the three, uncaring I left Jonny and my brothers behind. Within ten seconds, I lost sight of the butterfly and swore under my breath when I reached the sidewalk. I bumped and shoved through a handful of people, but same as two nights prior, I fucking lost her in the crowd.

Hands on hips and cursing under my breath while clenching a toothpick between my teeth, I stood alongside the street, scanning for a glimpse of red-brown waves.

Bikes rumbled by, and I recognized one of the blonde girls clinging to a biker's back. Sure enough, the third bike carried my little butterfly. She, too, wrapped her arms around the biker's waist.

Someone's old lady, I told myself as they drew near, deflating my cock. *Fuck.* A one-percenter, The Silent Demons, our fucking rivals, I noted as the first bike slowly passed by. I shifted my gaze back to the third bike as a slew of curses flew past my lips. Why them of all fucking people? Why not some random biker hitting Sturgis for the first time?

Butterfly's gray-green gaze landed on me.

My breath caught, and I stared back, everything stilling around me, falling to a hush in my ears like in a fucking movie. I couldn't have torn my gaze from her if I'd tried. An electrical current of awareness and fucking lust simmered the ten feet or so between us as the bike her thighs hugged slowly rolled past.

She turned her head, her gaze flitting down over me and back up as I stood, hands still on my hips, unmoving except for the throb in my cock. A smile lit her eyes, and she fluttered her fingers at me as the biker turned right, taking her away.

Janie

Every single hair on my body stood on end the second my gaze landed on the bearded badass alongside Sturgis's main road. Hands on narrow hips, a scowl marring his lips, but those eyes. Hazel and bright, the man peered at me with an intensity that made me want to bend over, grab my ankles, and beg him to take what he wanted.

God.

I clenched my thighs together, wishing a vibrator buzzed between my legs rather than Cal's Harley I straddled behind him.

I turned my head, keeping the leather-wearing hottie in sight as long as I could. A Fallen Glider, according to the "67" tattooed on his neck. A member of the one club that hanging with would lead to all sorts of trouble.

Unable to give a shit about boundaries in my manic state, I fluttered my fingers at him seconds before Cal turned, taking the fine piece of eye candy from view.

Lower lip between my teeth, I contemplated the hottie biker all the way back to our hotel, every cell of my body on fire and wanting to take flight. Countless bikes passed us in the hot sun beating down on South Dakota, the dry air chapping my face. Closing my eyes brought the man's face vividly to my mind. Strong nose and cut cheekbones. But those *eyes*! I wanted him like I hadn't wanted a man in a long damn time.

Tall, broad shoulders, tight leather pants with a bulge worthy of drool—and an ass clench at the thought of him burying his thickness deep inside.

Damn.

Soaked panties, no vibrator at the hotel, and a shared room with my two best friends…

My body tingled with the need for a good, hard fuck with the Fallen Glider my mind had become obsessed over with one eyeful.

Tasha and Lori hopped off the back of the bikes Cal and I had followed, and soon I stood beside them, waving as the three bikers drove off. They were our rides while enjoying our first time at Sturgis Motorcycle Rally.

"I need a nap," Tasha said and yawned.

"You need to tuck those tits away before your dad sees," Lori said with a snicker while pointing to Tasha's double-D's spilling from her bikini top.

Tasha stuck out her tongue and slid the triangle of material back over the nipple that had escaped.

"You okay, Janie?"

I blinked at Lori and rubbed sweaty palms on my jean shorts, trying to slow the thoughts flitting through my brain. "Did you see that biker as we left? Tall, dark hair, full beard?"

Lori's brow rose. "There are thousands of bikers here. How the hell—"

"Hazel eyes intense enough to flutter a girl's heart?" I added. "Toothpick between his teeth. Bulge that would soak any woman's panties? Well, almost every woman." Images of him flashed behind my eyelids as I blinked.

"Wanna go back and find him?" Tasha asked before I could spout off more praise, still checking to make sure her tits were covered. "See if he's up for a little three-on-one action?"

Her lopsided smirk as she glanced up through her long, dark lashes pissed me the hell off. If I found Hottie again, I wasn't interested in sharing that was for fucking sure. And, with him being a Fallen Glider...

"Nah." I shook my head and faked a yawn while starting toward the hotel's entrance, my steps quick.

"Too much beer last night."

"Shit," Lori muttered, "you're not kidding. My head is still pounding."

"Wait up," Tasha said from behind me. "When you're on a high, you never feel hungover. Ever. If anything, you're even more of a raving lunatic."

"Shut it, bitch." I elbowed her as she drew alongside me, even though I knew she wasn't making fun of my illness.

"Normal would have been better, but I'm glad you're flying right now, Janie," Tasha hugged me with one arm as we stepped into the air-conditioned hotel lobby. "Otherwise, Sturgis would suck ass."

"Would have been a total waste," I agreed, thinking of how much I struggled to even open my eyelids during one of my depressive episodes.

"At least our dads finally agreed to let us come out here," Lori said while pushing the button for the third floor. "We've been begging for what? Five years? I love ya and all, Janie, but I'd have left your ass at home if you'd been in one of your shitty moods."

"Fucking twenty-three," Tasha said, ignoring Lori's declaration, "and our dads finally admitted that we're women, no longer little girls that need constant care and protection."

"Maybe they'll actually let us start dating," I muttered with a frown, my mind on the hazel-eyed hottie with the big package between his powerful-looking thighs. Little did our dads know that all three of us had snuck out countless times since turning eighteen, hitting every dance club we could weasel our way into—all because of my need for excitement and my girls' desire to help me deal.

"My dad says I'm not allowed to date until I'm thirty," Tasha said, flicking her long, bleached-blonde hair over her sunburned shoulder.

"My dad still thinks he can choose my husband for me," Lori said, followed by a snort.

I'd never found someone interesting enough—or enticing enough looks-wise—to tempt me. Sure, I'd given up my cherry, just like my friends, to men we didn't really care about. We'd all just wanted to lose our virginities on the same night. Since then, I'd had dozens of hookups that satisfied my lust while on a high, but always left me hoping for something more in the back of my mind.

Thank God our dads didn't know.

My body continued to buzz, my mind flitting from one thing to another as Tasha and Lori collapsed on the beds to rest. Since a manic episode had wrapped me up in its clutches for the previous couple of days, I'd brought along things to Sturgis to keep my brain occupied while normal people rested.

I booted up my laptop and, rather than work on the website I'd promised to have designed for one of my author friends before the following week, dove into the novel I'd been slaving over for two years. The words flowed, the romance taking a decidedly erotic tilt as Hottie's face continued to flit through my memory. The words kept coming from the voices in my head, telling me how awesome their story was, how I was the only one who would tell it—and do it justice.

I kicked ass—even though I knew once the cycle turned, I'd hate everything about the story's evolving into heat and angst. One extremely hot scene later and grinning ear-to-ear, I put the novel aside and pulled up my photo editing software, my knee bouncing non-stop under the small table I sat at.

A quick download from my phone, and I scrolled through my pics from Sturgis. A half-hour later, I'd edited a few dozen and created two collages to post on social media.

"The fuck you doing?" Tasha asked from the bed behind me.

"Working on my book and photos."

She grunted, and I listened as she pattered to the bathroom.

"How ya feeling?" Lori asked, her blankets rustling behind me.

"Awesome." As though I'd downed countless shots of espresso, my body continued to buzz. "Wait'll you see these pictures … and the sex scene I added to my book." Grinning, I turned around and spilled all of the awesomeness I'd accomplished while my friends had slept.

****

Once the sun set, we had our babysitters take us back into town so we could grab a late dinner. As usual, I had no appetite but forced down a small salad with grilled steak. My gaze scanned non-stop, every corner, every person, every bike that passed us as we made our way down the street after eating.

Tasha muttered a few times about my energy level as I bounced ahead of them, but I ignored her, my strides leading my arm-in-arm friends ambling behind me.

I caught a glimpse of hair shaved on the sides, longer on top … a taller-than-most man a few yards ahead of us. A rush of adrenaline flooded my system, and I hurried my steps, a smile stretching my lips.

"Wanna slow the fuck down?" Tasha called after me, not for the first time, but I shoved through the people in front of me, desperate to get to him.

"You know she's insatiable when she's like this," I barely heard Lori's reply. "Janie!"

I ignored my friends and plowed onward toward the wide shoulders and tattooed neck, my body tingling and agile enough I felt I could vault into the air, summersault, and land a perfect "10" in front of him. I fucking needed him.

Like, now.

"Shit!" I pulled up short, realizing the man I'd been hell-bent on following had disappeared. "Shit!" Turning around to my left, my eyes threatened to pop out of their sockets as my gaze jumped from one person to another—rapid enough to hurt my head. An almost complete circle brought my stance angled toward the picture window of a bar.

The place was packed, music and loud voices spilling from the propped-open door.

"It's wet t-shirt time!" someone with a microphone shouted from inside. Hoots and hollers quickly drowned him out.

Inner lip between my teeth, I craned my neck to scan the people inside.

There ... on a stool at the bar ... the hair, the shoulders. He turned his head toward his left and spoke around a toothpick to the man beside him.

Hottie.

All the blood in my body rushed down between my thighs, and I clenched my pussy muscles tight.

I glanced over my shoulder but couldn't see my friends.

"Fuck it," I said, my voice and legs shaking, my heart thumping. I grabbed my cell from my back pocket and shot off a text to Tasha: **I found him. Don't wait up for me.**

I strode into the bar without a thought of consequence for what I was about to do.

Hawk

"Here ya go." The bartender set a shot of whiskey in front of me, pulling me from reliving my life the past two miserable days since first seeing the little butterfly.

I dipped my head in thanks and downed my drink, my thoughts grim, half-depressed by the lack of fucks I had to give about almost everything except that little butterfly I hadn't been able to find since she'd driven away earlier that afternoon.

On top of the lack of fucking depressing me, our club numbers had been steadily declining across the States. If the drug business end of our club wasn't so fucking lucrative, Jonny probably would have shut our chapter down—and I wouldn't have blamed him.

Someone with a bullhorn announced a wet t-shirt contest, and while my brothers catcalled their appreciation of the coming contest, I sat waiting for another shot, a scowl on my face.

My fucking balls ached.

Young twenty-somethings climbed onto the other end of the bar. Buckets of water sloshed down over them as the male patrons continued to hoot and holler.

I returned my gaze to the empty shot glass in front of me.

"Goddamn, look at those tits," Jonny said, his voice loud enough I could hear him.

A glance up revealed the women parading toward us, one by one, their shirts plastered over fake and real tits alike as they stepped over sweating mugs and bottles. The woman at the bar's end, the final contestant from what I could see through the sashaying and jiggling bodies topping the wooden slab, had a long mane of red-brown hair.

I leaned forward, leaned back, trying to catch a

glimpse of her face as my cock swelled at the thought of the little butterfly.

A break in the swaying bodies, and her gray-green gaze landed on my face. Flashing eyes. Wide smile. Joy and a whole lot of fucking lust.

Boom.

Just like fucking that, all blood raced to my cock. "Goddamn," I said, elbowing Jonny.

"The fuck?"

"It's her." I nodded with my chin toward where I'd seen the little butterfly, desperate for another glimpse.

"The woman you've been lusting after and keep losing in the crowd?" he asked with a laugh.

"Fuck you." I all but growled the word.

"You said she's a Silent Demon's old lady," Jonny said, his voice raised as he leaned toward me.

I shoved a hand through the long hair atop my head. "Yeah."

"You *sure* she's his old lady?"

I strained my neck, cussing about the crowd between my teeth. "Kinda young, so maybe not, but still. I'm not touching a Silent Demon's whore."

Another break in the action allowed me an eyeful of the woman who had my balls twisted into knots the previous two days.

Water poured down over her chest and the white tank clinging to her pert tits as she held her cell phone high overhead to protect it. The bartender dumped another over her chest, and butterfly's dark nipples strained against the soaked fabric.

Lips parted, she turned and followed the parading women ahead of her, tucking her phone in her back pocket. Like a proud peacock, she pranced along, her eyes clear, unfazed by alcohol.

"Fuck." I growled again, glaring at the men

packed in the bar, knowing they lusted after butterfly's perfect rack. "Fuck!"

Jonny shot a glance at me as the second woman in line leaned down and shook her tits in his face. "The fuck is your problem?"

I stood, my hands fisting against my thighs, unable to explain the jealousy raging through my body, pumping adrenaline through me.

My cock didn't give two fucks the little butterfly was an untouchable or that her man might be in the crowd whistling after her. The fact she was off limits to me made my balls ache all the more. I needed to get my dick wet, the sooner the better. A warm, willing hole…

I adjusted myself but couldn't get rid of the fucking scowl denting my brow.

Butterfly drew closer, her tightened nipples and juicy ass snaring my glare as she spun and tossed her hair. Her gaze never left my face. That fucking silence muffled everything as we stared at each other.

The other contestants hopped off the bar to my left in my peripheral vision, but I only had eyes for the little butterfly.

Still standing, hands still fisted, I waited as she drew near, knowing my life teetered on some fucking cliff.

Her smile widened, and she stepped right off the fucking bar without hesitation, falling toward me.

My arms reacted before my brain processed she'd thrown herself at me, and her softness landed against my chest. Her sweet breath fanned my face as I drowned in her sparkling eyes. The subtle scent of apples filled my nose.

Fuck the world and fuck my life. I needed a taste.

I took her mouth, demanding entry with my tongue the second her soft lips touched mine. I saw fucking stars. Thrusting in brought a groan to my chest, and she yanked hold of my hair while wrapping her legs around my waist.

One hand palming her ass cheek, the other fisting in her long hair, I devoured her mouth, mimicking what my throbbing cock wanted to do between her thighs. Plundering every inch.

Mad fucking lust.

Someone slapped my back. "Take it someplace else," Jonny hollered as the bar's racket filtered through the ringing in my ears. "We won't be back to the hotel for a couple hours."

I tore my lips from hers, panting, my entire body shaking. "Do me a favor, Jonny," I hollered to him. "Crash in Digger's room tonight."

The little butterfly stared up at me, moist lips swollen, eyes wide but still twinkling.

"Let's go."

I read her lips more than heard her over the continued catcalls and hoots. She slid her legs down from my waist, but I wasn't so quick to release my hold on her ass.

Lacing her fingers through mine, she flashed a dazzling smile up at me. She moved toward the door, tugging me along.

I shot a glance at Jonny.

He lifted his shot of whiskey, a grin I hadn't seen for a long fucking time lighting his eyes. "Enjoy!" he hollered.

Fucking planned on it.

Turning, I allowed her to lead me out of the bar and into the night.

Janie

My heart thumped in my chest, and I fingered my lips while shoving through the bar's crowd, the taste of Hottie still on my tongue. Goddamn, the man could kiss. My panties had to be soaked through, and the frayed jean shorts hugging my curves, too.

Pussy pulsing with the need for the hard length I'd felt pressed against me, I stalled out once we reached the sidewalk.

Hottie took over, tugging me to our left.

Giggling and shaking legs light, I hurried after his long strides. I didn't give two shits where he took me as long as he *took* me. Fast. Hard. In some dark alley, under a fucking streetlight … I just needed his cock deep inside of me. I'd always been crazy in my mind for excitement and sex while manic, but never with such desperation.

The Fallen Glider's logo on his back didn't even hinder my step or mindset. A sergeant at arms patch revealed more about his nature, but again, I didn't give two shits.

He climbed onto an old, black Harley and met my gaze, his hazel eyes sending another rush of moisture onto the soaked cotton strip of my panties. One brow cocked, he tipped his head, indicating I could climb on behind him.

My choice.

I didn't know his name. He didn't know me.

Body flushed through with heat, I laughed and threw a leg over his bike, wrapping my arms around him, my hands fishing beneath his flapped-open colors and tight, white t-shirt.

The beast rumbled to life, and he pulled away from the curb.

Hard abs met my wandering fingertips, up over

his huge pecs, down along the narrowed waist to the band of his leather pants.

Hottie reached the highway and tore off in the opposite direction of where our hotel sat. Closing my eyes and crowding close, I breathed in the scent of leather and his musky cologne as the wind whipped at my hair.

I reached between his thighs and slid my palm down over the hard cock nestled against his right thigh. My mouth flooded with drool as my pussy spasmed.

He sped up, and I grinned, my cheek smooshed against the Fallen Gliders logo on his back.

Every time a high caught me up in its clutches, I turned into a nympho, but nothing like the wildness consuming me. One thrust of his huge cock, and I would set off like a dozen fireworks exploding at once. A mere flick of his tongue...

I moaned and tried to rub against him—the bike vibrating between my thighs—anything to get me off. "*Fuck.*" I moaned again, so fucking close my toes tingled in readiness.

Hottie slowed, and I opened my eyes to find he'd taken us to another hotel.

He parked and shut off the bike, the sudden silence ringing in my ears.

I hopped off the bike and fought to not fidget in a dance to contain my need to come as he climbed off. At his full height, he easily towered over me by a foot.

"Come on," he said, grabbing my hand, his low voice rumbling and unsteady.

Biting my inner lip against the giddiness making my stomach flutter with giggles, I hurried after him.

He slid a card key into the slot by a door and pulled me in after him.

I should have been scared. Should have worried

I'd allowed a complete stranger—maybe a sicko murderer—take me back to his room, but I couldn't find a single fuck to give.

With a flick of his wrist at the light switch, the hotel room came into focus, but the next second, he yanked me against him, slamming me against the closed door.

An oomph left my lips, and he swallowed it down while devouring my mouth. My pulse raced as I wrapped my legs around his waist and ground my throbbing pussy against his cock.

Too many fucking clothes…

Hottie wrapped his arms around me and strode toward the bed, his mouth searing kisses along my jaw, behind my ear. "Christ, do you smell good."

He tossed me on the bed, and I bounced with a squeak and giggle, my gaze glued to his body as he yanked off his colors. I tore off my soaked tank and shimmied out of my shorts and panties as he ripped his t-shirt off overhead.

"Goddamn," he all but growled while pulling a condom from his back pocket. His gaze glued to my soaked folds, he shoved his leathers down to his knees. "Come here."

I scooted close, propping my feet on the edge of the bed, legs splayed wide. "Hurry." Lower lip between my teeth, I gripped the comforter alongside my hips and waited the agonizing three seconds it took him to roll the rubber down his huge cock. Thick, veined, and angry-red, but I didn't fear his fitting inside of me. I was a sopping mess.

He pressed the head of his cock against my opening and grasped my raised knees, gaze on my eyes. One fucking thrust seated him fully inside of me, bowing my back off the bed.

"Oh fuck!" I shrieked, my eyelids shut against the luscious burn, the invasion I needed more than oxygen.

He pulled out to the head. "Look at me."

Panting, hanging on by a mere thread to sanity, I did as told.

"I've been dreaming about fucking this cunt since I first saw you two days ago." Hottie slammed balls-deep into me again, and tingles raced up my legs as I clutched the comforter. I held his gaze, lost in the lust shimmering in his eyes. "Burying myself deep inside of you." He pulled out, head and all before ramming back in. "Hitting your womb…" Another full-length thrust settled the tingles in my lower stomach. "Making you fucking mine."

"Fuck!" I shrieked and writhed as my climax stole my breath, my mind, my body.

His fingers bruised the insides of my thighs as he held me wide and slammed into me over and over, grunting and growling like an animal as my pussy tried to pull him deeper.

"Oh, God, yes!" I grabbed his wrists as another climax swept over me, arching my back. Head thrashing to the side, lips parted, I panted, heart racing.

"Christ!" he hollered and slammed deep, the head of his cock pulsing against my cervix.

"Oh, my God. My God…" I heard myself whispering between gasps of breath.

He growled and released his hold on my legs and leaned down, capturing my mouth.

Mind. Fucking. Blown.

I'm in deep shit…

He was still buried inside of me as his kiss turned languid, his tongue tracing the inside of my mouth, my lips as his hot, hard body rested against mine. He hummed as though enjoying the taste of me, his hands tangling in my hair as his lips and tickling beard trailed along my jaw again to nuzzle under my ear.

Heart still hammering in my chest, I ran my hands up his back and wrapped my shaking legs around his waist.

"Fuck." I groaned the word as a shudder rippled down through me.

He felt so fucking good inside of me, pressed against me, the scent of male and sex swarming my nose.

Lifting onto his hands to plank above me swept air-conditioned coolness over my sweat-dampened skin. A slow smirk wrinkled the tanned skin at the corners of his beautiful eyes.

"You're gorgeous," I said, lifting my fingers to his beard.

"So are you," he murmured, his low voice an aphrodisiac to every cell in my body.

His cock remained hard and against my womb as we stared at each other in the silence.

My mind gained control over my body again and began to race—all good things. Wild thoughts, images of his fucking me every which way from Sturgis all the way back east.

"I've been calling you little butterfly in my head since I first saw you..."

"Janie," I answered his unasked question.

"My brothers call me Hawk."

I raised a brow and smirked. "What's your real name?"

"Shit." He tensed for a second and backed off a bit, pulling half his length from my pussy. I squeezed my inner muscles, desperate to keep him inside of me. His turn to raise a brow as he slid deep once more.

I moaned as a shudder rippled through me. "Don't distract me. Tell me your name."

"Robin."

Slapping a hand over my mouth didn't stop the giggles.

He frowned, pulled out, and slowly pressed back into my soaked, sensitive pussy.

"Robin," I breathed his name, still smiling as I tugged him down by the back of his neck.

"Hawk," he stated, staring into my eyes and thrusting again.

"I'll call you whatever the hell you want as long as you keep fucking me like this."

A growl rumbled his chest as he pulled away, leaving my pussy gaping and grasping at nothing.

"What?" I sat up.

"This fucking condom won't take another ball's worth of my cum." Hawk yanked up his leather pans around his thighs and stumbled toward the bathroom.

I laid back, grinning like a fool who just allowed a complete stranger to fuck her like the world was about to end.

"Shit." I scrambled for my jean shorts and grabbed my cell phone from the back pocket.

The toilet flushed as I shot off a text to Tasha while sitting on the edge of the bed again: **OMG he's amazing! Tell my dad I'm in bed if he asks plz?**

She immediately texted back a "yes" along with a heart-eyed emoji, and my shoulders relaxed. How many times had I covered for her ass?

THANKS! I quickly typed as the bathroom door squeaked open.

"Everything okay?" Hawk asked, his cock still upright and bobbing against his lower abs. He'd stripped completely, and I trailed my gaze down over his powerful thighs, bulging calf muscles and back up. He held another condom in his left hand.

I licked my lips. "Yeah," I said, my voice scratchy and needy. "Just letting my friends know they shouldn't wait up for me." I tossed my cell behind me onto the bed and crooked my finger. "Come here."

He crowded between my spread thighs, and I grabbed hold of his ass cheeks, pulling his cock closer to my mouth. One swipe of my tongue over his slit, and he tossed the condom packet onto the bed beside me and fisted my hair.

"Open up, little butterfly."

I stretched my jaw, but his girth demanded more as he slid between my lips. "Mmm." Squeezing my thighs together at the rush of arousal, I peered up at him as he bottomed out against the back of my throat.

"Fuck," he whispered harshly, pulled out, and slid back in. "You look so hot swallowing my cock."

I relaxed my jaw and throat, allowing him to go deeper.

He groaned, and salty pre-cum coated my tongue as he backed out.

Wanting more, I tightened my lips around the head of his cock.

"Greedy," he murmured, pulling on my hair. "I like that." He rammed down my throat, and I gagged, instant tears leaking from the corner of my eyes.

"More," I whispered as he pulled away.

"Fuck." He held my head steady between his hands and gagged me again, his balls slamming against my chin, wetness without doubt smearing mascara down my cheeks.

I moaned encouragement around his cock and released one hand from his ass to slide my fingers down over my clit.

"You want to come again?" he asked while fucking my tonsils.

"Mmm," I hummed around his length.

He pulled his cock from my mouth and shoved me back with a hand between my breasts. Dropping to his knees, his face disappeared between my thighs.

"Oh, God!" I grabbed hold of his head and wrapped my legs around his shoulders as he lapped up the wetness coating my swollen folds.

His tongue rimmed my asshole, lifting me off the bed.

"Fuck, yes…" I groaned as he licked up through my slit to my clit, his soft beard sending shudders down through me. He flicked my clit with the tip of his tongue and wrapped his lips around the throbbing nub.

I shattered as though I hadn't had release in months, squeezing his head between my thighs, my fingers yanking on his hair as I tried to fuck his face.

Gasping for breath, I didn't want to release my hold on him, but he was ten times stronger than I was and pulled away.

"On your knees, butterfly."

God, yes … again. Pulse thrumming and mouth dry as a bone, I flipped over, pressed my chest into the mattress and stuck my ass up in the air.

One thrust buried him inside my aching pussy, and my brain fuzzed at the edges as he fucked the ever-loving shit out of me.

****

Spent and boneless, I slumped onto the mattress and curled on my side as Hawk once more left me gasping for oxygen, cold air pebbling my sweaty skin. Satisfied and for the first time not wondering if there might be more, I lay like a corpse except for the rapid rise and fall of my chest.

Eyes closed. Lips smiling. Goddamn, Hawk knew how to use his cock. I couldn't turn off my brain, though.

I wanted him again even though my body actually didn't want to move. The memory of his hard cock thrusting into me … the warmth of his skin covering muscular, tattooed pecs I wanted to lick…

He collapsed onto the bed beside me, and a warm, wet towel slid over my bare pubic bone. "Lift your leg over me," he murmured.

Took me a second, but I draped my leg over his hip.

"Was I too rough?" he asked, his tone and touch gentler than I'd expected for the way he looked and fucked.

"I liked it."

"You sore?" he asked, tossing the washrag aside and pulling me snug against his entire length.

"Not really." Still smiling, I slid my palm down over his bearded cheek. "You turn me on so damn much, two of you could fit inside of me."

His brow shot up.

I laughed, betraying the jitters still fluttering in my stomach, making my brain race, and making my words sound rushed. "Not really, but you know what I mean."

"Yeah." He spread his fingers across my lower back, holding my pelvis tight against his. The warmth of his exhales bathed my face with his sweet breath as we stared at each other. "Been to Sturgis before?" he finally broke the comfortable silence I fought not to fill. Can't have him thinking I'm a lunatic after one single night. God knew I wanted way more than a quick fling.

"Nope. This is the first year that me and my girlfriends actually hopped a plane and made it here rather than just talk about it." Considering what club he belonged to, I wasn't about to tell him the truth about how our dads had never listened to us beg to go with them the previous five years.

"Earlier today…"

"Yeah?"

A frown dented his brow. "You were on the back of a Silent Demon's bike. You his old lady?"

I laughed to cover the twist in my stomach. "No. They were just some guys who took us back to our hotel."

Hawk's body released the tension I hadn't realized held him. He smiled and let out a heavy breath, snuggling me closer.

"Do you have an old lady waiting for you at home?"

"Hell, no."

"Thank God." I couldn't contain my smile. "Where is home?"

"New Hampshire. You?"

"New York."

He slid a tangle of my hair over my shoulder and slid his fingertips down my chest to circle one nipple, his gaze on my hardening nub. "We're pulling out the day after tomorrow."

Like a crack of lightning, pain raced through me, tightening my throat. "That soon?"

"Yeah."

I swallowed, and he lifted his gaze to my face again. "I really want to spend more time with you."

"Same here."

He bit down on his lower lip.

"What?" I asked.

"This is going to sound crazy…"

I lifted one eyebrow but couldn't tear my gaze from his perfectly bowed upper lip.

"Will you let me take you back to New York?"

Blinking didn't help me find any teasing in his

eyes when I jerked my attention up. "Like, ride across the country on the back of your bike?"

"Yeah." He rubbed his thumb over my tight nipple, waking another tingle between my thighs. "If you get sick of me, or just plain want to go home, I'll get you a plane ticket to JFK at the nearest airport."

Jitters woke inside of my stomach as my mind took off down another path rather than fucking Hawk again. How to get my shit from the hotel, what to tell my friends, how to sneak off without being seen by anyone. The thought of not doing what he suggested didn't even cross my mind.

"Yes."

Hawk all-out grinned, and I rolled him onto his back, climbing to straddle his hips. "And what if I end up driving you insane?" I asked, breathless with excitement. "Gonna toss me off your bike at the nearest rest stop?"

"You already drive me insane," he said, his voice the lowest I'd heard as he grabbed my hips and moved me over his hardening cock.

My turn to smirk. "You know what I mean."

Nothing but seriousness filled his eyes. "You radiate a joy I've been missing out on. Life sparkles in your eyes. Your smile. I'll never grow tired of either. I'm going to sound like a fucking sap, but you lit up my life today, Janie, and I want to see where this can go."

Knowing what lay in my future, regardless of the meds I swallowed down every morning, dissolved that smile he stared at.

"What?" he asked, rubbing his thumb over my bottom lip.

"I—I've never had anyone tell me something like that before."

"Nothing I hate worse than lying. I'll always be honest with you, little butterfly."

Wanting to ignore the niggling of nerves and shame in my stomach, I ground myself against his cock hard enough he grabbed hold of my hips again. "And what do you want right now?" I whispered, leaning down so my lips hovered an inch from his, knowing my eyes twinkled with the life he'd spoken of.

"To fuck you until you can't see straight."

"Mmm. Yes, please."

Hawk

Her tight, soaked pussy had clamped around my cock and milked me dry for the third time in three hours. Yeah, I'd wanted to claim her puckered rosebud hole before night's end, but her greedy cunt was like the sweetest drug to my system. Couldn't fucking get enough. And the mewling sounds coming from her full, parted lips and the wildness in her eyes as she came...

Fuck.

I shifted on my Harley as she clung to my back, her hands in constant movement sculpting my abs and chest as I drove her to her hotel at the ass-crack of dawn. I'd never acted so spontaneous and devil-may-care-ish in my life.

She was no man's old lady, though. Free as a bird and seemed to want me just as much as I did her. A fucking nympho, and I'd told her so. She'd claimed to have these urges on occasion that no one had been able to satiate—until me.

I grinned like a fucking fool. Mad lust ... mad everything. Jonny was going to ask what the fuck I'd gotten into, and I didn't have the words to explain what I felt. The dizzying effect of Janie on my brain, the way she overrode all common sense, the way her *life* literally brightened mine.

No fucking way was I letting her go.

My grin remained as I pulled into her hotel's parking lot.

She hopped off, her gaze flitting around the parking lot and dozens of parked bikes. "See you outside One-Eyed Jacks at noon?"

I nodded in agreement to the plans we'd made before crawling out of bed a half-hour earlier.

Smiling and walking backward, she fluttered her

fingers. *See you,* she mouthed, and I pulled back out of the parking lot, feeling as though I'd left my heart in her hands.

I returned to my hotel, set my phone's alarm for eleven-thirty, and crashed—a smile still plastered on my face even though I didn't even know her last name.

****

Skin-tight jeans plastered to Janie's legs, heeled boots made her at least three inches taller, and a jade-green tank brought out the green in her eyes. A baseball cap pulled low on her brow, her hair in a thick braid over her shoulder—fisted in her hand as she stood fidgeting in front of One-Eyed Jacks. Her face lit up, and she dropped her hand from her hair as I rolled past her on my bike and our gazes collided.

Once I found a place to park, I strolled back toward her, grinning like a fool. "Hey."

"Hey back," she said as I stepped into her personal space but didn't touch her rocking body.

"You look so good, I want to fuck you right here, polo-shirted police asshole over there be damned."

She giggled, glancing at the rent-a-cop. "Pretty sure we could find a dark corner or a bathroom somewhere."

"Naughty, naughty girl."

Purring under her breath and running her hand up over my pecs, she leaned into me. "You have *no* idea."

I grabbed her hand and kissed her palm. "Ready to ride?"

Her eyes twinkled. "Yes."

"Let's go."

Hand firmly clasped in mine, she followed the short distance to my bike. Sure, I would have loved nothing better than to go back to the hotel and fuck until we passed out, but I wanted to get to know Janie better.

Burrow into her brain and not just her body. See if there was common enough ground to build that something I hoped I'd found.

She'd turned her baseball cap backwards and clung to me as we rolled up Route 90, the wind and warmth bringing the comfort of home as my Harley rumbled under us. Her fingertips traced the muscles of my upper body under my t-shirt, and my fucking cock throbbed. No way in hell we'd make the scenic loop I had planned without fucking her in the woods somewhere.

Once in Spearfish and heading south down the canyon highway, I slowed down and enjoyed the towering ponderosa pines growing out of solid rock and the limestone walls rising around us. Dozens of bikers had fled Sturgis as well, enjoying the wildness of the Black Hills.

I headed up into Deadwood, and we stopped at Hickok's for a cheeseburger. Settled into a black barstool and beer ordered, I filled my eyes with the woman who'd been driving me insane since first seeing her.

She'd left her hat with the bike, and her red-brown braid hung to the middle of her back. Sunglasses propped on the top of her head held back the wisps of hair the wind had pulled loose in the wind. Pink tinged her cheeks, and as usual, a smile twinkled in her eyes.

"So, what do you think so far?" I asked her as the bartender set our drinks in front of us.

"It's so beautiful out here. Wish I'd come out sooner rather than just chatting about it with Tasha and Lori."

"Perfect timing, if you ask me." Slot machines behind us dinged and clinked with coins along with the din of players and other diners, but I couldn't pull my focus from Janie if I'd tried.

Her phone chimed, and she pulled it from her back pocket. A slight frown furrowed her brow as she read the message and replied, her fingers flying over the screen.

"Everything okay?"

"Yeah," she murmured, but her voice didn't convince me.

"Running off with some strange biker … I'd be scared for you, too."

Her head jerked up. "Who said anyone's scared?"

I shrugged and took a swig of my beer. "If your friends were any friends at all, they would be."

"Anyway." She shoved her phone back into her pocket and gave me a look that shot the blood straight to my dick. "Where we headed next?"

"Rushmore."

"I'd rather find a room somewhere."

Chuckling, I shook my head. "No rooms available around here for miles."

"There's plenty of woods around here…"

"Waiting will make it even better." I told her what I'd been telling myself the past hour.

She blew a heavy breath between her lips. "Yeah, I suppose you're right."

"Rushmore so you can say you've been there, then we'll head back to Sturgis." That damn gleam lit in her eyes again, and I groaned into my beer. "You're like the worst drug, you know? I've gone too long without a hit."

Janie leaned toward me, her warm breath against my ear. "I'm wet and willing…"

"Christ." My fingers tightened around my beer, but I wanted to build, not just fuck. "You know, I don't even know your last name."

She laughed and sat back in her chair to grab her

Coke. "Kincade. You?"

"Richards."

"Robin Richards," she murmured, her lips smiling against the rim of her glass.

"Hawk."

She giggled around her mouthful of soda, and I scowled.

"I told you my real name in confidence."

Her laughter continued, and I found myself smiling along. For a woman to change my mood like a light switch, she could damn well call me whatever the hell she wanted.

Janie

"Okay, *Hawk*," I said once my giggling subsided. "You've had your face buried between my thighs, but let's do the whole twenty questions thing so we won't feel like strangers." Not that I had an issue with fucking the delicious stranger beside me, but like he'd said he wanted to see where this could go, and I was definitely on board—even if the fucked-up truth about our situation couldn't possibly end well. Hell, I'd lied about my last name … and would without a doubt lie again if needed. Anything to keep him close for as long as I could.

"You first," he said.

A knot had twisted my stomach from Tasha's text letting me know my dad had begun to worry about me. Again, she'd covered for my ass, but I feared my anxiety would cause me to crash, ending whatever had started between Hawk and me.

"How old are you?" I asked.

"Thirty-eight."

"Shit."

His brow rose. "Have an issue with my age?"

"I'm only twenty-three."

"Shit."

We both laughed. "I don't give a fuck if you don't," I said, leaning toward him again, wishing I could crawl onto his lap.

His bright, hazel eyes peered at my face, a soft smile wrinkling the skin at the corners. "I *don't* give a fuck."

Less than two inches separated us, and I hovered close, loving the tension that zapped between us. "What is this, Hawk?" I asked.

"I don't know, but like I said last night, I sure as hell want to find out."

"You're serious about driving me home?"

"Dead."

And when I crash... "I'm looking forward to it," I said as our burgers arrived. "How long have you been with the Fallen Gliders?" I asked a few minutes later, continuing our game.

"Going on close to twenty years."

I knew the answer to my next question, but curiosity over his stance opened my mouth. "Is it true what they say about the whole brotherhood being first, family second?"

Hawk shrugged and finished chewing a bite of his burger. "For the most part, yes."

"But?"

A furrow appeared between his eyebrows. "Seems like the times are changing. Brothers leaving. Less tolerance from the law..." He shrugged again.

"And where do you stand on the whole brothers versus family thing?"

The burger in his hands held his attention as I waited. "It's always been brothers first for me because I've never found a reason to think otherwise."

Giddiness tickled my stomach. If he didn't take off at the first sign of my crash, maybe, just maybe the star-crossed-lovers feeling in my gut would turn out okay.

We continued with our question game, even though I had to shade the truth here and there about who and what I was. Turned out, he wasn't the prying type, and we ended up spending most of the time discussing our favorite HBO show that had been cancelled way too damn early for either of our tastes—*Deadwood*.

Since I'd always wanted to see the real streets where Sheriff Bullock, Calamity Jane, and Hickok himself had strolled, we ended up footing it for a while, fingers laced between us. Still flying high even with the niggling of anxiety lacing my stomach, I pulled him from place to place, snapping selfies of the two of us, blowing my money on all sorts of tiny, useless trinkets I could fit in my bag, and pulling deep-seated laughter from him on more than one occasion.

Making him smile, hearing him laugh, being that light he said I'd brought to his life, became my mission, and I thrived on the thrill of curving his lips.

An hour later—and having learned Hawk was a mechanic with his own shop, his retired father lived in Florida with his long-time girlfriend, and he'd buried his mother years earlier—same as me—we set out for Rushmore.

I hadn't told Hawk the truth about my mother's death, but I rarely told anyone the fact the shit eating her mind had enticed her to hang herself. Inflicted with the same crippling mental illness, I understood all too well the depression, the voices in her head that led her to make the choice to leave me and my dad. It'd been ten years since she'd gone—ten years since I'd been diagnosed. Since then, countless highs and lows had come and gone, but I'd never once hungered for the continued high to last like I did while holding onto Hawk as we rode through the Black Hills.

Like fingers grasping at water, I tried to hold on as we peered up at the four faces of dead presidents until we headed back north, the sun sinking to our left.

I lay my cheek on Hawk's back, the leather cool on my hot cheek as I snuck my hands beneath his t-shirt. Hot, hard skin met my fingertips. His stomach muscles flexed under my touch, and I slid my hands up higher, over the swell of his pecs.

My pussy throbbed, and as usual while I was manic, I wanted to fuck. I should have enjoyed the entire day—and I did to a point, seeing one of America's must-see sites—but Hawk's nearness, the sexual tension between us even while just chatting, had me wet and willing like I'd told him.

He'd seemed more interested in watching me while I checked out Deadwood and Mount Rushmore, and I couldn't help my smile over that fact. Awareness of his hazel-eyed gaze tingled over my skin time and again all day long until I trembled with need.

"I want you," he'd whispered in my ear as I stared up at good old Abe.

My answer had been to grab his hand and head back toward the bike.

We sped north, a smile on my lips, his body tense against my front. I never wanted the emotion and high I rode to end.

Ever.

It took fucking forever to get back to his hotel. We weren't in the door for ten seconds when he dropped to his knees and yanked my jeans to my ankles. He buried his face in my soaked pussy, his groan and lip-smacking tipping my head back against the door, my fingers fisting in the longer hair atop his head.

My climax tingled up from my toes, and I yanked Hawk's ravishing mouth away from me. "I want to come around your cock."

He stood and started stripping, revealing tanned, smooth skin, tattooed pecs and that luscious V leading into his leathers. I didn't waste any more time but tore at my bootlaces and the jeans hindering him getting between my thighs.

Bared from the waist down, I threw myself on the bed and spread my legs wide, beckoning with one hand. "Hurry."

I bit my lip to keep from giggling as his fingers

shook while ripping at his leathers and rolling on a condom.

Green fire lit in his eyes as he climbed onto the bed between my thighs. One thrust seated him against my womb, tearing a shriek from my lungs, same as the night before.

"So fucking wet for me." Planking over me, he thrust a half-dozen times as I dug my nails into his bulging biceps, and he worked in and out of me, stretching me to fit his girth. "Goddamn, butterfly." A few grunts and groans, and he slowed, gyrating his hips to rub his pubic bone against my clit.

"God, right there." I moaned, my head tipping back and eyes closing. "I'm so damn close … don't stop!" My climax slammed into me with Hawk's next thrust, sizzling my skin, frying my nerve-endings in exquisite torture. I couldn't catch my breath, couldn't focus through the euphoria singing through my blood.

Hawk pulled out and flipped me onto my stomach before the pulsing in my pussy ended, yanked my legs closed, and one thrust landed him against my womb again. I screamed into the mattress, my hands fisted in the comforter as another climax toppled over me.

I couldn't squirm, couldn't lift my hips to meet him. I was at his mercy, the mercy of a rutting beast who slammed into me again and again, holding me down with the full weight of his sweating body.

"So good, so fucking good." His thrusts became sporadic, his breaths ragged. "Fuck!"

His cock pulsed deep inside of me, and gasping for breath, he relaxed, his hot breath on my ear. "Fuck. I could die a happy man right now." The rumble of his low voice seeped into my back, clear through to my chest, and I smiled. It seemed I couldn't do much more than that when with Hawk.

A heaved breath, and he pressed up onto his palms, sliding his semi-hard cock from between my legs.

While a shuddering sigh melted me like hot wax into the bed, my mind continued to buzz. Had he somehow cured my mood swings? I'd never flown so high for so long.

The touch of a warm, wet cloth between my thighs slowed my mind and brought me back to the present. I spread my leg wider, giving him access to the mess I'd made while coming around his cock.

"So pink … still swollen. Goddamn, you're beautiful." Hawk kissed each of my ass cheeks before dipping down to place a chaste kiss on my pussy.

I rolled and stretched, peering at him beneath my lashes.

Hawk sat beside my hip, naked as a jay, his hair a mess, cheekbones tinted pink. His gaze slid down over my body and back up as though savoring the sight of a juicy steak. Heat filled his eyes as they rested on my face.

"Changed your mind about taking me back east tomorrow?" I asked as he peered down at me.

"Never."

I smiled, although I knew it was the perfect time to tell him the truth about who I was—what I was—and save us both a shitload of heartache. I couldn't bring myself to do it. I couldn't bear the thought of ending something that had just begun. Maybe my meds would offer control for a change. Maybe the crash wouldn't bash me over the head like a hatchet, robbing the life from me. Maybe, just maybe, Hawk would be the kind of man who could handle the craziness inside my head.

Hawk brushed my braid over my shoulder and slid his fingertips along my collar bone, down between my breasts. "What's going through your mind?"

"I'm scared."

"I won't hurt you."

Physically, I didn't think he would, but my heart?

"You're the happiest, most spontaneous woman I've ever met. I want you on the back of my bike, Janie. I want to give us a few more days. Please."

My throat swelled, and tears stung my eyes, but not the kind that arrived with a bout of deep depression. I scooted close to Hawk, and he stretched out beside me, gathering me close against his hard chest.

"Kiss me," I whispered an inch from his lips.

Soft and gentle, reigniting the fire inside of me no man had been able to quench while I rode my high. Our mouths grew greedy, tongues twining, tasting, and fucking.

"I want you again." Hawk's groaned words along with the hardness of his cock against my thigh brought a whimper up from my chest. He reached behind him, grabbed a condom from the bed stand, and handed it to me while lying back.

I straddled his hips, tore the packet open with my teeth, and eyed his thick cock. "It's amazing these things fit," I said, rolling the condom down over the flared head of his dick.

"I hate the fucking things."

"Me, too."

Hawk grasped my arms and pulled me over his body. "Fuck me, little butterfly."

A few gyrations of my hips, smearing my wetness over his length, and I shifted to notch his flared head inside of me.

The whiskers on his jaw twitched as though he clenched his teeth, and he palmed my hips as I pressed back onto him, stretching my pussy, filling myself with every inch of his cock. We both groaned as he bottomed out against my womb, and he wrapped his arms around me, capturing my mouth.

A euphoric thrill shot through me, as though all the planets in every galaxy aligned, every star behind my eyelids shining brightly. Like a shattering zap of lightning, I felt Hawk in every pore of my body, his taste, his touch searing my nerve endings.

I panted against his mouth, overcome with emotions and feelings I didn't understand, but the steady thrust and retreat of our fucking, the gasps and moans accompanying the slick, hot friction between our bodies built to a frenzy. It overshadowed all thought, until all I could do was feel. Exquisite torture of the best kind, growing excitement as the edge of a cliff drew closer.

Wetness coated his thighs—my thighs—as I rubbed against him, in frantic need to sprint forward and throw myself into the unknown. My clit throbbed, and every thrust of his powerful hips rubbed me against his pelvis, heightening my need.

Hawk's hold on my hips bruised, but the pain only intensified the wildness consuming me.

"I'm going to come," I heard myself pant through the ringing in my ears. "Don't stop. God, please…"

His hips pistoned, thrusting his cock into me, and I clung to his body, my fingers fisted in his hair.

Each breath brought me closer, every slide of his throbbing length deep inside of me curling my toes, sweeping tingles up through to my stomach. My lungs failed me as my body finally leaped over the edge, pulling me into oblivion.

Hawk groaned as my pussy clamped around him, but he didn't come, didn't stop until I lay lax on his chest.

He flipped me like a ragdoll onto my stomach and yanked me onto my knees. I stuck my ass in the air, still trying to catch my breath, my ears still ringing.

The bed dipped between my thighs, and he grasped my cheeks, spreading me wide. His hot tongue shoved into my asshole, and I squeaked, but he held me tight. "Anyone claim this tight, little hole yet?" he asked, his voice shaking as he slid the pad of his thumb through the saliva he'd left behind.

"No."

"I want to bury myself inside your ass." The tip of his thumb slid past the ring of muscles, and I gasped at the burn.

"You can have it. Please," I whispered, my eyes clenched shut against the renewed need raging through me again as he slowly worked his finger inside of me.

"Goddamn, you're tight." He shifted and grasped my hip in his free hand. "Tonight, I'm going to finish off in this lush, swollen cunt."

Thumb still inside of me, Hawk pressed into my pussy with his cock, filling me like I'd never been before. "O-oh, God…"

My breath caught, and like a rubber band pulled tight, my limbs tensed. He pulled out and thrust back in, his thumb rubbing against my inner wall, and I snapped. Cum poured from me as I groaned like an animal into the pillow.

"Fuck me, Janie. That's it, baby."

Body moving on its own, pressing back to meet every thrust of Hawks hips and hand, I took what he offered, never wanting it to end, needing the rush sweeping through my blood to send me into a fucking coma.

Hawk slammed into so damn hard I slid forward, and two more grunted thrusts swelled his cock inside of me. He shuddered, his dick pulsing, sending another tingle through my limbs. Once again, he relaxed against me, his chest heaving, breath heavy in my ear.

****

An hour or so later, we fucked one more time, the pizza we'd had delivered wiped out, the box tossed to the floor. The spice of pepperoni lingered on Hawk's tongue as languid thrusts into my mouth and pussy brought on a climax that left me boneless.

Still hard, he'd carried me to into the shower where he washed every inch of my weary body.

I slid to my knees, and he fucked my tits I held squished together, finally shooting his cum up over my face. I fucking loved it.

Darkness had fallen, and when we finally rode down the highway toward my hotel to get my bags, I realized Hawk had completely sated my appetite. Contentment wrapped me in a fleece cocoon and kept me smiling even though possible trouble awaited at our destination.

I'd texted Tasha to let her know I was on my way to grab some of my things, but she hadn't responded before we'd left. Both Tasha and Lori didn't like my plan—or the lies they had to tell until I headed east on the back of Hawk's Harley—but they'd agreed earlier that morning when I'd snuck into our hotel room to cover my ass, wanting me to enjoy myself for as long as possible since all good things always came to an end for me.

Hawk parked his bike at my hotel's rear entrance, and I hopped off, my gaze flitting around the near-empty parking lot. "I—I'll go grab my stuff. No need for you to come up."

"You sure?"

I wiped my palms down my jeans. "Yeah. Be right back."

Hawk

I sat back and relaxed the best I could while checking out her swaying ass and those creamy thighs I couldn't wait to get between again.

Hot and tight… The memory of her slippery cunt swelled my cock again even though the spent balls beneath ached like a motherfucker.

She disappeared inside, and I pulled out my cell.

"Our room still smells like satisfied pussy and cum," Jonny said by way of hello.

I chuckled. "Can't say I'm sorry."

"I just got back. Where the fuck are you?"

Heaving a sigh, I glanced at the door Janie had disappeared through. "At her hotel, picking up her things."

Silence.

"I'm taking her with me tomorrow when we leave and dropping her off in New York."

"The fuck, Hawk?"

"I know, right?" I scratched the back of my head. "It's out of the way, but … I don't know, Jonny. She's … fuck. I don't know."

"You sound like Nicky."

"Fuck." My hand dropped to my lap. Our best friend had handed in his colors a few months prior, headed north, and found himself a younger woman who ended up claiming him in every way possible. "I don't believe in love, let alone love at first sight."

"I don't either," Jonny grumbled, "but you sure as fuck are acting just like him. Mel's got Nicky so wrapped up that the bastard still won't return my calls or texts."

Mine either, I didn't bother reminding him.

Nicky had left the Fallen Gliders because we dealt the opioids his sister had OD'd on. While I hated the fact he'd left us, I could understand his desire to distance himself. Fucking sucked, though.

He'd left, and I ended up filling the void he'd left in the club as sergeant at arms. "Can't stand the thought of leaving here tomorrow without her," I said, fighting to hold back a sigh. "Hoping by the time we should split from you for New York, she'll have agreed to come home with me."

"Shit." Jonny's heavy exhale hit my ear hard. "I think you're fucking nuts, but if she's the one you want right now, then she's the one you want. I've got your back—same as always."

"Thanks, man."

"You done fucking for the night, or should I go crash in someone else's room?"

My grin returned. "I've already blown my load three times."

"You're Hawk 'fucking' Richards with an endless supply of cum, or so the club whores say. No fucking way you're done for the night."

I laughed and rubbed my chest at the foreign feeling tingling there. "Yeah, well."

Jonny chuckled again. "I'll crash next door with Digger just in case you can't keep your cock in your boxers."

"I don't wear any fucking underwear."

"So that's your secret? Maybe I should give it a try."

Laughing again, I hung up and tucked my cell back into my pocket. Jonny complained as much as me about the lack of fuckable women in the club the previous couple of months. Not too many knew he struggled with getting his rocks off. He blamed age, but at forty-two, a mere five years older than me, I knew he lied.

He'd grown bored, same as I had. His brain was overrun with worry over the club and the declining numbers. The fine line we walked between being one-percenters and hating the crisis our drug dealing enabled.

No fucking way we could change, though. The presidents' meeting a few nights prior had spelled that out clear as shit.

Fallen Gliders supplied what people wanted. We made money, and unless we handed in our colors, we'd do so until six feet under.

"Fuck," I muttered to myself, eyeing the hotel's back door. Pushing aside the dismal thoughts, I turned my mind to Janie.

Full of life, exuberant, spontaneous Janie. A cool, spunky glass of water on a sweltering day. The sweetest rush of fresh air from an ocean breeze.

Goddamn, am I fucked.

The thought didn't turn my stomach, didn't sent a shot of worry or the desire to flee through my body. Snagged on her line, she had me by the balls. Aching balls.

I doubted I had a drop of cum left in me, but my dick didn't give a shit. I wanted to slide into her cunt again and again until I passed out.

She hurried out the hotel door, her baseball cap pulled low on her forehead, long hair still in a braid over her shoulder. Lower lip between her teeth, she glanced around the parking lot. Like a squirrel with her tail on fire, she scurried toward me in a new pair of skinny jeans and her riding boots, two small bags in one hand and a large backpack slung over her other arm.

"Your friends give you shit?" I asked while flipping open the saddlebags on my bike.

"Not too much. Tasha promised to take the rest of my stuff home." She shoved things from the bag into one side, then arranged the rest into the other. "Let's get out of here before they change their minds."

A whisper of unease snuck into my brain, but I pulled away from the hotel, Janie's heart thumping fast against my back as she clung to me.

I opened it up and sped back down the highway, buzzing by other bikers and the occasional car even though it had to be close to one. We arrived back at my hotel, and Janie seemed to have chilled the fuck out, smiling and eyes flashing again.

"Tired?" I asked as she set her backpack on the floor.

"Nope."

"Oh, how I envy the young and their boundless energy," I said with a chuckle before leaning down to brush my lips against hers. "We're leaving at six. Best get some sleep."

She sighed as I pulled away. "All right."

Twenty minutes later, she crawled beneath the sheets and curled her naked body around mine.

I groaned at her soft warmth pressed against me and turned on my side to face her. "No fucking way I'll sleep with you all pressed against me like this."

"Mmm." She rolled over and snuggled her ass against my groin. "Better?"

"Fuck, no," I said between clenched teeth. Thoughts of her virgin, puckered hole swelled my cock.

"You can take me again," she said, her voice all sultry and lust-laced as she wiggled against me.

"I want this ass," I said, trailing a fingertip between her cheeks, "but that's going to take some time. Time we don't have right now." I lifted my fingertip to my nose and inhaled the musky scent of her. "Goddamn, woman, do you tempt me."

She giggled and fucking wiggled again.

"Go to sleep, little butterfly. I'll satisfy your craving for my cock tomorrow."

A huffed, exaggerated sigh, and she pressed her back against my chest. "Promise?"

"Promise. Now close your eyes."

Took a long time with Janie fidgeting beside me, but I eventually gave over to the exhaustion from having drained my fucking balls.

Janie

Light snores emitted from Hawk's lips, and I still stared through the darkness of his hotel room, wide awake, the sheets chafing at my skin. Sure, my body felt like it had been used hard and put to bed wet, but my mind wouldn't stop.

Lori hadn't said shit when I told them Hawk was taking me back east. Tasha had helped me pack, her giddiness and constant stream of jealous words giving me the confidence and guts to stick with my decision.

If they knew that Hawk belonged to the Fallen Gliders, they would have locked me in the room in order to save my life. Dad finding out who I rode off with would put us, both Hawk and me, in a grave, I didn't doubt.

My choice to accept Hawk's offer was selfish in the worst sense of the word, but I'd never wanted something so badly in my life. I would soak in his attention for as long as I could because God knew, if I crashed and he saw the real me, he would drop me fast as fuck.

I finally drifted off, and the second I opened my eyes to early morning light hinting around the blinds, I took stock of my racing mind, my emotions. My yawn morphed into a smile.

Safe for another day.

Hardly rested, but ready to face the day, I fought to keep still since the dead weight of Hawk's arm lay over my waist. Like a furnace, his body let off amazing, luxurious heat that soaked through my skin.

Unable to help myself, I stretched, thinking about the day ahead.

Hawk's cock stirred to life, and he tugged me back against his chest. "Morning." His low voice rumbled in my hair, tingling between my thighs.

"*Good* morning," I corrected him, still smiling.

"No such thing until I have a few cups of coffee in me."

I pulled away and tugged on my jeans, his declaration giving me a mission.

"Where you going?" he grumbled, blinking as I hurried to dress.

"To get you some coffee."

"Are you always this smiley in the morning?"

I laughed. "No, but I woke up beside the hottest man on the planet, and I want him just as awake and full of life as I am."

He cursed and pulled my pillow over his head.

Still snickering, I grabbed his keycard from the table beside the door and let myself out of the room. Gathering my messy hair into a ponytail, I hurried to the lounge. Free coffee and Danishes—just like I'd expected. Two Fallen Glider bikers sat at a small table, hunkered over their coffee. Hawk's brothers. I offered a big smile when they glanced at me and poured my hottie some coffee.

I glanced at the sugar and creamer packets. He seemed more like a black kinda guy. I grabbed a cherry Danish for Hawk and decided I'd better get myself one even though I wasn't hungry.

Hungrier than I thought, I devoured the damn thing in less than five bites on the way back to our room.

Ours. Damn, I liked the sound of that.

"Coffee and a cherry Danish!" I said as the door clicked shut behind me.

Hawk pushed up to sit against the headboard, the sheet falling down around his waist, revealing the sculpted muscles of his chest and stomach.

"You are so fucking fine," I said, handing him the

coffee and Danish and trailing my gaze down over him to the tent between his thighs. "And this cock." I snaked my hand under the blankets and wrapped my hand around him. "So thick, so—"

"Goddamn, Janie." Hawk thumped his head against the headboard twice as I slid my hand down over his hard length.

Someone pounded on the door, and I yelped and jerked away from Hawk, my heart in my throat, adrenaline flooding my bloodstream. "Ten minutes, Hawk!"

"Fuck off, Jonny!" Hawk shouted back.

"Ten minutes or you're on your own!"

Hawk grumbled for a few seconds while I fought to chill the fuck out. I'd thought for sure Dad had found me.

"You okay?" he asked a few seconds later while swinging his legs off the bed.

"Yeah." My voice came out breathless, and I forced a smile. "Gonna go brush my teeth and get ready to roll."

He nodded and sipped his coffee. "Want me to put your backpack with the laptop in Digger's truck so you don't have to take it on the bike? He's following behind us with everyone's bags."

"Oh, that'd be great. Wasn't looking forward to wearing it across country."

We made it out the door in twelve minutes, my lips thoroughly kissed, traces of Hawk's cum still in my mouth. "Tonight," he'd murmured while pushing my ass out the door, "this is all mine."

God, yes…

The thought of having a cock shoved up my ass had never sounded appealing before, but after having Hawk's thumb buried deep inside of my virgin hole, I wanted it all. Every sordid desire, every sick way imaginable—my body was his to do with as he pleased for as long as my high stayed.

Everyone was already on their bikes, so I didn't get to meet his friend Jonny before climbing onto Hawk's Harley behind him.

"Ready?" he asked over his shoulder as I wound my arms around his waist, my fingers finding their way beneath his shirt.

"Always," I replied, my grin wide, my mind crazy as a little kid hyped up on a dozen Pixy Stix.

Hawk squeezed my hand through his shirt, and we pulled out onto the highway in formation, heading east.

My face hurt from smiling—especially since I hadn't seen a text from either Tasha or Lori before leaving with the sunrise. I couldn't even begin to imagine the shit that would fly when my dad found out I'd taken off with some random guy.

Since I'd lied, at least my friends didn't know his real name—or the fact he sported a "67" tattoo on his neck.

Forcing into oblivion the thoughts that fact brought to mind, I fought to contain the wiggles wanting to sweep over me from pure giddiness.

Sitting up, I stretched my arms out wide against the wind, my giggles uncontainable.

Freedom on the road. Freedom from Dad and all his rules. Freedom to make my own choices—fuck the consequences. My high couldn't possibly get any higher.

****

We stopped a few hours later to coffee and gas up. I hopped off the bike, my legs itching to take a quick sprint around the gas station. Hawk chuckled at me as I tapped my foot waiting for him to fuel his bike.

"So this is the young woman who has your balls twisted in knots."

I turned toward the smiling voice and found the man who'd been sitting beside Hawk in the bar the night I'd joined in the wet t-shirt contest. "Janie," I said, holding out my hand.

"Jonny." His dark-eyed gaze lifted over my shoulder as he released my hand. "If this fucker gives you any shit—"

"Fuck off, Jonny," Hawk grumbled.

"—you let me know and I'll make sure you get on a plane the second you're ready."

I could feel the annoyance in Hawk radiating over my back and couldn't help but laugh. "And if I annoy the shit out of him?"

Jonny's chocolate-brown eyes twinkled as his gaze returned to my face. "I'll make sure your ass is on a plane taking you far away from my brother."

A threat without being a real threat. *Be nice to my friend, or else…*

I winked. "Gotcha."

He turned away, and my breath caught as my gaze slid down over the back of his vest.

The fucking president … shit. My foot started tapping again.

"Did you even sleep last night?" Hawk asked while grabbing my hand and starting toward the entrance behind his friend.

"A couple hours." My damn voice shook.

"You gonna crash and fall asleep on the back of my bike later today?"

My heart seized, and I jerked my head up to peer at him.

He smiled through his beard, happiness shining in his eyes.

Crash. As in exhaustion. Yeah. My smile felt forced. "Nah. I could conquer the world today."

A low chuckle, and he shook his head, pushing through the door.

Twenty minutes later, bellies filled with coffee and junk food I'd forced down my throat, we headed out once more. Shimmers of heat waved over the asphalt in the distance, but cruising through the air brought a decent enough breeze we didn't sweat.

My mind focused on the night ahead, the chance for Hawk to own a part of me that no man had ever touched. I couldn't wait.

****

We ended up having to share a room with Jonny since they'd only booked enough rooms in advance for the same number of men that had driven out to Sturgis. There was no room in the inn for a couple in need of privacy. Half-clothed, horny as hell, and limbs tangled, Hawk and I whispered late into the night.

I shared some about my family but kept the truth of what my dad did—what he was—to myself.

Hawk owned a small-engine shop a few blocks from the club that kept him busy and out of trouble, and when he learned I knew enough about a two-stroke engine to rebuild one from scraps, he about shit himself.

It came from spending hours working on bikes with my dad. I told him that much, at least. Just not whose shop we toyed around in.

I didn't sleep worth a shit—at least, not that I was aware, but in the morning, my manic high remained, and I grinned with the hope that Hawk had miraculously cured me.

Same as the morning before, I hurried to the lounge to get him coffee. I pulled my cell from my back pocket and powered it on. Knowing it would ring and ding like crazy once Dad found out I'd taken off, I hadn't bothered turning it on at all since last I'd texted Tasha.

Sure enough, dozens of messages and texts, but I flew too high to give a shit. Without listening to or reading any of them, I slowed my steps and shot off a quick text to my girls and then my dad, letting them know that I was fine, that I would see them all back in New York in a few days. That done, I powered it back off and shoved it into my pocket, a huge smile on my face and bounce in my step.

Hawk

My fucking balls ached to the point riding my bike hurt. We pulled into our hotel for the night and thank *Christ* they had extra rooms.

After a quick fuck against the wall to release the sexual tension that had been riding us for almost forty-eight hours, we collapsed on the king-sized bed, Janie giggling. She lay on her side, eyes shining in the sunset's rays since I'd been too caught up in her to bother pulling the shades before sinking into her tight cunt.

Still breathing heavy, I tucked wind-blown strands of hair that had escaped her long braid behind her ear. "Did I hurt you?" I asked as the subtle apple scent of her shampoo or body lotion wafted over me.

"No." Her smile knifed me in the chest. "I like it when you're rough. Never been slammed against a wall like that before. Gotta say … it was hot as fuck."

As always, her enthusiasm and happiness infected my head, and I found myself smiling in return. "Roll over, little butterfly."

"Mmm." With a smirk, she did as told, her plump ass drawing my attention.

I squeezed one cheek, kneading her with my fingertips.

"God, that feels good."

A grin widened my mouth, and I gave the other cheek the same attention.

"Can I ask you a question?" Janie asked, turning her head toward me as I used my thumb to massage her lower back.

"'Course."

"Have you ever thought of life outside your club? Like, would you ever leave, or are you a lifer?"

I considered her words for a few seconds as she

searched my face and I massaged slowly up along her spine. "The Gliders is all I've known since I became a member."

"So that's a no?"

Shrugging, I pursed my lips, my gaze roaming down her back along with my hand to her ass. "Sure, I've thought about what life would be without my brothers, but I've never considered leaving. Never had a reason to. Why?"

She mimicked my shrug. "What do your brothers think about you taking a near-stranger across the country on the back of your bike?"

"Don't give a fuck." I stilled my hand on her ass cheek, fingers splayed to hold as much of the soft flesh as possible. One swipe of my fingers along her cum-soaked lips from fucking against the wall, and I explored back up to rim her tight rosebud, ending all thought of serious talk. My cock twitched as her eyelids fluttered shut.

"I want this ass," I said, pressing a finger past her muscle ring.

Her lips parted and hips lifted as I went deeper.

I pulled out to my fingertip and slid back into the knuckle.

"Holy shit." Her half-mewled words sent a rush of blood into my cock.

Adding a second finger, I worked her tight opening, preparing her for my much-larger cock. She continued to let out those goddamn mewls, moans, and groans that drew up my balls.

Unable to wait any longer, I leaned down over her back while sliding my fingers from her ass. "Don't move," I whispered against her ear and climbed off the bed. A side pocket of my bag held lube and a large stash of condoms—same as every time I'd visited Sturgis. I grabbed what I needed and returned to find Janie gyrating her hips against the mattress.

I swatted her right ass cheek, and she squealed, jerking sideways. "I said to lay still."

"But I'm so fucking horny," she moaned, lifting her hips and sliding her knees under her.

Puffy, pink, and wet, her cunt called out to my aching cock. The sweetest drug, but I'd made up my mind to claim her virgin hole.

"I ought to swat your other cheek for disobeying me," I said, biting back my smile.

"Mmm." Janie wiggled her hips.

I hauled off and landed another swat, my handprint blooming red within seconds of her squeak. "Like that, do you?"

"Maybe," she answered, more than a little sass coating the word.

My fucking hand shook as I lifted the wrapped condom to my mouth and ripped it open. Sheathed and lube in hand, I crawled between her spread thighs.

Her breath caught as I dribbled lube down between her ass cheeks.

"I'm going to fuck this ass so damn hard, you'll be feeling me for days." Hands pressing her cheeks together, I slid my cock up through, coating my length.

She panted and grasped at the sheets above her head.

I slid two fingers in deep again, lubing her up good for me. Groans and gasps fled from her lips as I took my time stretching her hole.

Once she trembled on edge, I wiped my fingers off on the sheets and grasped her hips. "Ready, little butterfly?"

I didn't wait for a reply but pressed the tip of my dick against her hole. She groaned as I pulled her back toward me, stretching her puckered rosebud until I breached the tight ring.

"Fuck, that burns." She gasped as I worked in another inch. "Goddamn."

Jaw clenched and fingers digging into her thighs, I fought to keep from shoving deep inside of her. I pulled out that inch and pushed back in again, gaining a little more ground.

Those damn mewling noises bled from her lips as I backed out to the head. "Okay?" I asked, my voice as strained as my balls.

"Y-yes." She gasped again as I slid in deeper. "Don't stop."

"Not going to." Twice more, I retreated and pulled her hips back as I pressed in, finally seating myself balls-deep inside of her ass. "Christ, are you tight," I said between clenched teeth.

"Move ... Hawk, please." Her fingers grasped at the sheets as she tried to move against my hold on her hipbones, every inch of her quivering skin covered in goosebumps.

I pulled out to the head and finally allowed myself to thrust.

"Fuck." She ground the word out as I angled my hips and repeated the motion. "Oh, fuck!"

"Like that, baby?" I asked while thrusting deep.

"Fuck, yes!" She flipped her head to the other side, tendrils of hair lying across her cheeks, fluttering with each exhaled puff. "Harder."

Goddamn, this woman...

Always aiming to please, I did as told, my balls slapping against her sopping pussy.

She arched her back and lifted her ass higher, like a fucking cat in heat.

I grabbed hold of her braid with my left hand and

lifted her head, the sound of our skin slapping like the high of a plummeting rollercoaster rushing through my ears. Her ass cheeks jiggled with every thrust, and I held on tight to her hair, jerking her back against my pistoning cock.

Balls tightening, sweat beading on my brow—she needed to fucking come so I could blow my load.

I released my hold on her hip, and she continued to fuck my cock as I swatted her jiggling ass cheeks.

Rather than squeak, a deep groan rolled past her parted lips, her eyes clenched shut as I reddened both of her cheeks.

"I need you to come so hard." I half growled the words and reached around to slide my fingers through her wet cunt. Her swelled clit protruded, and a quick rub between my slippery fingers sent a shudder down through her body.

"Fuck!" My little butterfly shrieked, her ass clamping down on my thrusting cock.

"That's it, little butterfly … goddamn, your cum is dripping off my balls." I glanced down at my lubed cock slamming into her ass over and over, holding off my own climax as her cum dripped onto the mattress.

Janie writhed beneath me, panting and moaning as I continued to thrust deep into her ass. "So damn good. Fuck."

"Give me another," I said, rubbing against her clit again. "Take me over with you."

A low whine built in her chest, and she arched her back as an animalistic groan flew past her lips.

I growled. "Fuck, yeah. Just like that."

Her ass clamped down on me again, and I closed my eyes, giving over to the climax rushing from my balls. Toes digging into the mattress, hand tangled in her braid, I shouted my release. Every deep-seated thrust, every squirt of cum into the condom sent stars shooting across the back of my eyelids. "Goddamn … fuck." One last tremor shuddered through me, and I moved with Janie as she sank onto the bed.

We both panted for breath, and I pushed up onto my elbows to keep from crushing her, my forehead on the mattress beside her head. Buried to my balls in the hottest, tightest ass I'd ever fucked. My head wrapped up in the most beguiling, addictive woman I'd ever had. My heart losing itself to the butterfly I couldn't get enough of.

Sweaty heat emanated between her back and my front, and I pressed my lips against her apple-scented hair. "You okay?"

"Mmm."

Unsure if her murmur meant yes or no, I pulled out with a sigh. "Don't move."

"Couldn't if I tried," she said, her voice muffled against the mattress.

On weakened legs, I made my way to the bathroom, cleaned myself up, and grabbed a warm, wet towel.

Janie lay as I'd left her, sprawled on her stomach, legs spread, arms stretched but lax above her head. A small smile curved her lips.

Like melted butter, I thought while maneuvering her body in order to wipe her cum and the lube from between her thighs and ass. I wished I'd had some oil to rub into her red ass cheeks, but I liked my handprints marking her backside. My smile remained as I finally pulled the blinds shut, encasing us in near darkness, and climbed onto the bed, tugging the blankets over us.

Janie snuggled into me, and I wrapped my arms around her, holding her close. She fit against me like well-worn leathers, her sweet breath and subtle scent encasing me in sheer, fucking heaven.

No words. Just shared breaths until she breathed heavy and I gave over to the exhaustion pulling on my brain.

****

I woke to find only a hint of sunrise around the blinds. Soft curves pressed against my side, and I turned my head, searching for Janie's outline in the darkness. Rarely did I smile in the morning, but I found myself doing that exact thing while enjoying the moment, being present in the seconds slipping past as she continued to breathe deeply.

My cock tented the sheet as it did every morning, but I ignored it and focused on my need for coffee. I slipped from the bed, careful to let my little butterfly rest after being ridden so hard the night before. The memory of her tight ass and her cries as she climaxed shot hot lust through my balls until my shaft ached. Tucking my cock into my leathers brought a grimace to my lips.

She needs sleep, I told myself while tugging on my boots, not bothering to lace them.

I hesitated at the door, gaze roaming the curves barely outlined on the bed, but clenched my jaw and quietly let myself out.

Not yet six, and warmth lingered in the air, promising a scorcher of a day. Other than a big rig rumbling by on the highway a few hundred yards to the north, silence coated the flat, dry land.

A fresh pot of coffee dripped as I let myself into the motel's office/lounge. The three tables sat empty, but the half-full ashtray and remnants of stale smoke from whoever sat there last burned my nose like acid.

"Morning," the man behind the counter called as the door shut behind me.

"How ya doing?" I asked, not really wanting to

know as I made a beeline for the coffeepot.

"Damn tired. Hope you slept better than I did."

I made a noise in my throat he could take however the hell he wanted while pulling two Styrofoam cups from the stacked sleeve beside the bowl of creamer cups and basket of various sugar packets.

The guy behind me continued his one-sided chat while I stared at the drip, drip of the coffee. Occasionally, I tossed out a grunt of agreement even though I didn't hear half of what he said.

Record highs for the day, no chance of rain.

Had I heard the latest about the buffoon in the Oval Office?

Sports stats…

Seriously, I could care the fuck less, I thought while pulling the filled pot out and pouring into the cups.

At least I tossed a, "Have a good one," over my shoulder while leaving him five or so minutes later for the fresh, outdoors—and silent—air.

I filled my lungs before taking a sip of coffee, and my smile returned as I took another. Balancing the two cups in one hand, I let myself back into our room.

Light spilled from beneath the closed bathroom door, and a quick glance at the bed showed Janie had crawled from beneath the rumpled blankets.

The shower turned on before the door clicked shut behind me, and I sat Janie's coffee on the small table to my left while kicking off my boots.

I imagined her stepping naked into the hot spray, and my cock swelled again. Rather than join her, though, I sat on the edge of the bed, sipped my coffee, and clicked on the TV, immediately muting the noise. The news scrolled along the screen's bottom as I listened to the shower run, my mind far from headlines and stocks.

Was a handful of days too soon to fall for a

woman? I felt like a fucking giddy teenager with a massive crush—and no hope or desire to see it squashed. Janie filled up the empty parts in my life I hadn't realized I'd had. She brought happiness where it'd been sorely lacking for a long-ass time, like a rainbow over my head, giving off a burst of color in a dismal world.

I chuckled at the poetic thoughts in my head. A sap in love?

The L word didn't sit well. Never had, but I let the thought linger while drinking my coffee and waiting for Janie to finish up with her shower.

A muffled sound like a sob came from the bathroom, drawing my gaze to the closed door. Another similar sound brought me to my feet, and I rapped on the door. "Janie? You okay?"

I frowned as a sure sob reached my ears. Without thought or hesitation, I let myself into the bathroom.

"Janie?"

She cried harder, and I tossed my coffee in the sink.

"Janie?" I asked again when she didn't answer and tugged back the shower curtain. She huddled against the wall, arms wrapped around her middle, hair unbound and dripping, hiding her face from me. Her ass still sported slight memories of my handprints, but the misery radiating from her kept my thoughts on the present.

What the fuck...

I climbed into the shower, uncaring of my leathers and t-shirt. "Janie, what's wrong, baby?" I asked, reaching for her.

She shied away from me, but I wasn't having any of that shit. Unyielding, she stood like stone as I wrapped my arms around her. The shower spit hot water against my shoulder, soaking me as I craned my neck to see if she'd hurt herself.

I'd taken her too hard the night before. Fucked her ass like she was one of the club whores rather than a young, tender woman to be treasured.

Goddamn you, Hawk, my mind whispered, clenching my jaw. *Motherfucking asshole.*

Half-keening cries spilled from her lips, and my chest ached at the sheer desperation of her voice, the depression slumping her body.

Fuck. I closed my eyes, tightened my hold on her stiff body, and rested my chin on the top of her head. "I'm so fucking sorry, Janie. So goddamn sorry."

She didn't respond, but only cried harder.

Unsure of what else to say, I kept my silence as the steam and heat filled the bathroom until I sweated.

Janie

I'd woken to a blanket of heavy darkness, the kind of emptiness I'd become well-acquainted with since my mother's death and my diagnosis. At least Hawk hadn't been lying beside me, waking to find me crashed into the pit of hell.

Knowing I probably didn't have much time, I forced my aching, exhausted legs to move and half-stumbled into the bathroom, desperate to escape the sure heartache to come once he returned.

I bit my fist at the first sob, but the second escaped. A soft knock and Hawk's gentle voice calling my name brought the fucking tears on full-force. Unstoppable. Unrelenting.

He stepped into the shower with me, fully clothed, and I tried to curl in on myself, needing to shield myself, the truth of my illness that would ruin the best thing I'd ever found.

Warm arms, steady heartbeat against my ear … but no peace.

Sure he would leave once he learned the truth, I continued to hold myself from clinging to him while my sobs echoed in the damn motel bathroom.

He would put me on the first plane. Never call, never text, just like every other guy I'd snagged for a few days.

Although he apologized—God knew what for—nothing could stop the stream of tears until they ran dry.

In silence we stood, me unyielding, him in soaked clothes, his body like an oven around me even though the bathroom filled with steam. He rubbed my upper arm and half-rocked me like a baby until I quieted.

I wanted him to leave without saying a word. I wanted him to kiss me, make the shroud of shit over my brain and heart disappear.

"Janie?" he questioned, pulling away slightly.

I kept my head down, but he tipped my chin with a finger until I relented. My gaze latched on his mouth, and I refused to look any higher.

"What's wrong, baby?"

Lips pursed, I shook my head.

"Did I hurt you last night?"

I shook my head again.

"Then what?"

"I—I can't..."

"Did you wash yet?" he asked when I didn't finish my thought.

I shook my head.

Hawk unwrapped the small square soap provided by the motel, lathered his hands, and took his time caressing every inch of me, not lingering on my breasts or between my thighs like I'd expected—and didn't want him to.

Once crashed, my body had zero desire for a cock, let alone a man touching me in a sexual way. As though my thoughts had snagged in glue, I couldn't process, couldn't make any decision if I'd wanted to.

The world had lost its color for me. Everything had dulled, the edges of my world blurring.

A small bottle of shampoo provided the bubbles Hawk worked through my hair, every gentle touch tightening my throat again. I refused to meet his eyes and closed mine when he encouraged me to tip my head back into the spray.

Once finished, Hawk pulled me toward him again, his hands on my hips, his hard chest and thighs pressing against me.

"Want to get out of here and have some coffee?" he asked a few minutes later as the steam continued to rise, the hot shower spitting at us both.

I managed a nod but kept my head down, my arms wrapping around myself the second he released me and stepped out of the shower.

Hawk held open a towel, and I stepped out, my legs shaking. As though all my energy and fuel had been drained over the previous couple of days, I fought to stay upright as he wrapped me in the length of rough cotton. I didn't care about anything—the dripping water, the squeak of the nozzle as Hawk shut off the water, him peeling off his soaked clothes and knotting a towel around his hips, the cool air that licked over my skin when he opened the bathroom door. I clutched the towel tight across my breasts as my nipples pebbled.

"Come on," he said, grasping my elbow and encouraging me into the main room.

I stood a few feet from the bed, swaying and staring at the floor while listening to Hawk rummage in my bag. Hell, I didn't even give a shit that he might come across my wallet and ID with my real name I kept hidden in the bottom.

"Leggings and t-shirt okay?" he asked, holding the clothes in my line of sight.

I nodded.

"Want me to help you dress?"

"No," I managed to whisper.

Hawk sat on the edge of the bed while I dried off and dressed, my movements mechanical in the darkness coating my brain.

Withholding the truth would only lengthen the looming, heartbreaking goodbye. Even though I'd hoped that maybe, just maybe, he liked me enough to stand by my side through the shit, I knew the plummet I'd taken would be too much.

Although I wanted to curl back up on the bed in a

fetal position and plug my ears, I remained on my feet and ran the towel over my damp hair one last time.

"I got you some coffee," he said, coming close enough his feet came into my line of sight, "but it's not too hot now. Want it?"

I shook my head, lower lip between my teeth and listened as he went to the bathroom and discarded the coffee.

"I crashed," I whispered the second he returned to my side, needing to get it over with before the tear factory started back up.

"What?"

"My high fucking ended, and this is my low." I forced myself to look him in the eye. See for myself the rejection so I wouldn't have any lingering hope.

Concern filled his face as he searched mine, skin creasing between his brows. "I don't understand."

"My neurotransmitters and circuits are all fucked up, just like my mom's."

"What can I do to help?"

No trace of disgust. No curl of the lips. No stepping away as though needing to put distance between us lest he catch my mental illness. He stepped close and rested a palm on my hip.

Tears filled my eyes again as hope he didn't just misunderstand flitted through my brain. I couldn't be so lucky.

"There's no cure, but I take meds to help lessen the swings," I whispered, thinking of the bottles with my real last name buried in the bottom of my bathroom bag. "Sticking to a schedule seems to help me, too." A huff of tear-filled laughter puffed my lips as I hugged myself tighter. "Crossing country like this and staying up all hours of the night definitely didn't help."

"I'm glad you did."

Four words—not the ones I expected to hear. I actually smiled for real even though the black shroud still smothered me.

Hawk pushed my hair over my shoulder. "So this is your low."

I nodded, focusing on the scrolled tattoo on his chest.

"Are you feeling depressed?"

"Worse than you can imagine." Again, my voice came out as a breathless whisper.

"I've dealt with a bit of depression lately. Not that I know what you're experiencing, but we'll do whatever you need to feel better, all right?"

My heart ached, and more tears filled my eyes, wavering the image of his water-pebbled beard.

"Want to get something to eat?"

I shrugged while drawing a somewhat fortifying breath.

"Tell you what—" Hawk glanced at the door leading outside as though he could see through it, his hands lifting to massage my upper arms. "We'll spend the day here. Rest and relax. Maybe take a dip in that nasty pool out front."

"What about your brothers?"

"We were going to split off from them eventually to take you back to New York, so we'll just split a little earlier than planned."

"You're sure?"

"Dead."

Tears slid down my cheeks, but I held my heart and head in check. If my fucked-up head ran its usual cycle, he'd be sick of my blah, sometimes pissy nature before day's end. "M'kay."

Hawk cradled my head in his hands and swiped the tears from my cheeks with his thumbs. "I'll go talk to

Jonny, then we'll see about getting some breakfast."

"I'm not hungry."

He kissed my forehead. My nose. "I know the depression makes you feel that way, but your body needs fuel." I opened my mouth to argue, but he gently kissed my lips. "You're going to let me take care of you, little butterfly."

I nodded, and he turned away.

Twelve hours earlier, I'd have been salivating as he bared every inch of his skin to me and bent to retrieve new, dry clothes from his own bag.

Another wave of sadness slammed into me, and I sank onto the edge of the bed. Eyes closed, I let myself down onto the mattress and breathed a deep sigh.

"Be back in a few, baby."

I nodded that I'd heard, and the door clicked shut behind him.

At least I didn't feel all combative and bitchy like I sometimes did when crashing after such a manic high. My father always let me beat on his chest and scream—half of the shit I spewed from my lips I couldn't ever remember. He never spoke of it. Just held me until I slumped into a pile on the floor, and he'd put me to bed.

Dad.

More tears, more twists of agony in my stomach.

Without a doubt, I'd find myself back in New York all too soon—by plane—a slumped, tears-dried-up husk of the vivacious woman Hawk had been so attracted to.

More tears slid from my clenched eyes to drip onto the flat pillow beneath my head. I pulled my knees up to my chest and hugged my shins, giving over to the unrelenting, depressing thoughts.

Hawk

Fucked up neurotransmitters, she said...

I considered what Janie must suffer from while shoving my hands into my jeans pockets and making my way down the walkway to the third door down from ours. Her high had drawn me in while in Sturgis, but I refused to let her low spit me back out, leaving us both alone again.

Her body language had tried to shut me out, protect herself from being tossed aside as I'm sure most men would do at signs of her instability. But I wasn't some little boy ready to move on to the next fuck. A real man, a seasoned one with enough baggage of my own to drop her jaw, I wasn't about to leave her behind.

Janie needed me, whether she knew it or not. I might not be some smart psychologist or doctor who could cure her—if there even *was* a cure—but I sure as hell knew how to be loyal and stand beside those I loved.

The damn L word again.

I shook my head although the thought of actually falling in love with Janie didn't twist my stomach in knots. Inhaling until it hurt, I rapped on Jonny's door.

It pulled open a few seconds later by a rumpled blond-headed giant, bleary-eyed and scowling.

"Digger," I said, rather than good morning since I knew all too well he hated everything about the sunrise.

"The fuck you want?" he asked while scratching his balls through the boxers sitting on his hips.

I glanced past him at the two empty, twin beds. "Jonny around?"

"Went to the office for coffee."

Dipping my head, I backed up and started toward the office without another word. While I was known to need coffee in order to function in the morning, Digger often wanted to bash heads in before finally getting his paws on a mug. Best to leave him be until he had two or three cupsful sloshing in his empty stomach.

Jonny poured coffee into cups when I entered the office again. He glanced over his shoulder as the office manager called another greeting my way. "Still able to walk?" Jonny asked with a grin as I drew close.

"We need to talk," I said without cracking a smile.

His lips flat-lined as he nodded. Without a word, he handed me a coffee and poured another.

I followed him back outside and toward his room.

"What's up?" he asked and raised one of the cups in his hands to sip.

"If it's all right with you, Janie and I are going to stay on here for a day or two."

His brow lifted as he glanced over at me. "What's up?" he asked again.

I heaved a breath. "Long story short, I think she's bipolar. Has it bad and crashed this morning."

"Crashed as in depressive episode?"

I nodded. "Your sister is bipolar, isn't she?"

"Aubrey is, yes. Is Janie on meds?"

"Yeah."

Jonny handed me one of the coffees in his hands and opened his room's door.

The room smelled of sweaty feet and shit.

"Turn the fucking fan on!" Jonny hollered at the closed bathroom door.

"It's on!" Digger hollered back.

"Then open the fucking window!" Jonny put Digger's coffee on the bed stand between the beds and motioned at one of the chairs on either side of the small table beneath the room's front window.

"Can't stay long."

"Sit your ass down," Jonny said when I hesitated, pointing at the chair, his dark eyes flashing. My best friend and brother had taken a back seat to the Fallen Gliders' president.

I sat.

"You ought to put her on a plane and send her home."

"Can't do it."

Jonny sat across from me, hands wrapped around his cup. "Why the fuck not?"

"Too far gone. I'm completely infatuated with her."

"Fuck."

The old Hawk, pre-Janie Hawk, would have nodded in agreement.

"She got your balls in a vise grip already?"

A half-smirk lifted my lips. "Something like that."

"Fuck." Jonny scrubbed a hand down his face and over the dark shadow lining his jaw. "It ain't easy living with someone like her."

I nodded, all too familiar with the stories he'd told me of his sister before their parents finally got her checked out and diagnosed. "I want to help her. I want to be her knight on horseback—or bike back."

"You sure about this, Hawk?" He ignored my attempts at humor, his steady gaze boring into me as though drilling the truth of the situation ahead of me into my brain.

"Yeah, I am. I'm going to help her find her normal again."

Jonny sat back and sipped a few times, still studying my face. "We're pulling out after breakfast at the diner. Give me a shout if you change your mind before then."

"Will do." I stood and turned, more than happy to leave the stink of their room behind.

"Prop that fucking door open, will you?" Jonny said to me as I walked outside into the fresh, hot air. I chuckled to myself and dragged the heavy-ass chair between the door and jam in an attempt to air out the room like he'd asked.

"Oh ... hey, Digger!" I leaned back in the room.

"What?" he hollered from the bathroom, dragging out the word.

"When you get home, can you drop Janie's backpack at my place?"

"Yeah, now leave me the fuck alone so I can shit in peace!"

Chuckling and shaking my head, I made my way back up the walkway.

There was no question that I wanted to stay with Janie. Give her some time to level out a bit. A huge test early in our relationship—because I sure as shit had already decided she belonged to me. I just needed to get her to believe that I wasn't going anywhere that would take her from my side.

Fuck New York, I thought as I approached our door. She was coming home with me to New Hampshire, and I wouldn't take no for an answer. Mind made up, I let myself into our room. The TV flashed into the dimness, still muted from earlier. Janie lay on her side facing away from me in a fetal position. No sounds of crying reached my ears.

I kicked off my unlaced boots again and crawled onto the bed to spoon her from behind. She didn't pull away, but she didn't exactly melt against me like usual, either. "How ya doing?"

"M'kay, I guess." Her voice sounded scratchy, raw from the sobs she'd let loose in the shower.

"I talked to Jonny. Let him know we're saying on here until you're ready to roll again. Hope you don't mind that I told him about what you're going through. His sister is bipolar, so he totally gets it."

She nodded and finally relaxed in my arms. "You came back."

"Of course I did. I'm a loyal son of a bitch."

The silence stifled my mind as I considered all the ways I wanted to tell and show her what she meant to me. My cock had a mind of its own, swelling against the cleft of her ass, but at least I held myself in check, not thrusting against her softness like I wanted to.

I finally opened my mouth, needing to get on with my plans. "This is going to sound crazy—"

"Crazier than you wanting to drive me back to New York? Crazier than my fucking head?" She'd muttered the words, but at least she spoke without slurring or crying.

"I want you to come home with me."

She snorted but didn't move.

"I'm serious, Janie. You're like a tick burrowed inside my skin, except I don't want to pluck you out."

Still unmoving, she didn't respond for enough seconds my heart began to beat harder at the thought of losing her. "You hardly know me."

"I trust my instincts about people."

"I—I can't just up and leave my home."

"There's no man waiting for you in New York?"

"No."

"Work?"

She shook her head. "I do graphic design stuff from home since I can't hold down a nine-to-five job like a normal person."

"You *are* a normal person, Janie." I frowned. "A normal person with a mental illness."

"M-my dad will blow a fucking gasket," she said, ignoring my declaration.

"Then we'll go to New York so I can meet him and tell him you're coming to live with me."

She heaved a sigh.

"What?" I asked, rolling her onto her back so I could read her face.

She'd closed her eyes, and a furrow lined the skin between her eye brows. "Dad won't ever approve."

"'Cuz I'm a badass biker with a long beard, tattoos, and leathers?"

A corner of her lip actually quirked, giving me hope the wall of depression that had slammed on top of her would crack sooner than later. "Something like that."

"You're old enough to make your own decisions."

"Yeah."

"So that's a yes?"

She shrugged, and I relaxed onto the bed again, my head on the pillow beside her. I kept my hips away from her, trying to talk down my straining cock and aching balls. While depressed, I hadn't wanted a woman, so I very much doubted Janie had any interest in fucking.

We lay together for close to an hour in silence more than not as I asked questions about her illness and she answered.

She met with a psychiatrist on a weekly basis, had been hospitalized twice before being diagnosed, but had enjoyed a somewhat normal summer before the excitement of heading to Sturgis put her in a manic episode that had lasted longer than any she'd experienced.

The rumble of my brothers' bikes bled through the motel's thin walls, and I listened as they drove off together.

"I hope you don't regret this," Janie whispered against my chest, having finally snuggled into my arms.

"Never." I kissed the top of her head.

"Shit," she said, stirring to sit.

"What's wrong?"

"My backpack … I need to finish up a website I've been working on."

"Fuck." I grimaced. "I asked Digger to drop it off at my place when they got home."

Lips pursed, she lay back down. "Not like I can get the creative juices flowing while I'm like this anyway. I'll have to message her." Janie blew a heavy exhale between her lips, and silence settled over us again for a short time.

My stomach grumbled. "Ready for some food? I'm fucking starved."

"Nah."

"Mind if I head over to the diner and get some takeout? Be back in fifteen or so."

Janie shook her head, and I forced myself to leave the warmth of her soft curves. "Be back soon, baby. Call me if you need me."

Boots properly laced, I locked the door behind me and headed across the parking lot to the dive of a diner I expected we'd be eating at for the next couple of days.

Smoked sausages, corned beef hash, bacon, scrambled eggs, a pile of pancakes. *One of the boxes stacked in my arms ought to tempt Janie,* I thought twenty minutes later while heading back to our room.

She lay as I'd left her, silent TV still flashing.

I sat the boxes on the small table and flicked on the lights.

A grumble floated over to me.

"Got a ton of food over here. Bacon … pancakes." I opened the boxes and prepared two plates on the paper ones the waitress had provided for me.

Janie didn't stir.

I rounded the bed and scooped her up into my arms, ignoring her swat against my chest. "You need to eat."

"Don't want to." She pouted like a petulant child, but I set her on the chair.

"Just a couple bites, baby. I don't want you getting any weaker than you already are."

She heaved a breath, which lifted her slumped shoulders.

"If you don't eat, I'll take you over my lap and swat your ass."

I'd hoped for a glimmer of something in her eyes but got nothing. "Fine."

I dug into a pile of pancakes while she nibbled on a piece of crisp bacon.

"Did you take your meds today?"

"Not yet." She wouldn't lift her head to look at me.

"Are they in your bag?"

"Yeah. I'll get them after I'm done," she hastened to say. A handful of seconds later, she dropped the bacon back to the paper plate and started crying again. "I'm so fucking sick of this." Once more, her arms wrapped around her waist, and I hurried to chew my mouthful of food so I could offer some comfort. "I was doing well since May, and now *this*."

I leaned over and ran my hand from her shoulder down her arm as far as I could before the table hindered me. "We'll find your normal again."

She nodded, and I leaned back to take another bite.

"Pancakes are good," I said before shoveling them into my mouth.

With a sigh, she swiped the tears from her cheeks and picked up her plastic fork. She got five decent-sized bites down and a few swallows of OJ before I allowed her to leave me alone to finish the food.

Progress, in my book. A full day of rest, renting movies, and we'd see what the morning brought.

****

By our third morning in that damn motel room, I'd about had it with the stifling heat outside, the small room, and lack of … well, just about every damn thing. Fighting to keep my hands to myself had my muscles tense, my balls aching. Jerking off in the shower seemed like a shit thing to do, so I decided to tire myself out instead.

After coffee, I got down on the floor and did countless sets of sit ups and pushups. I went at it until my arms couldn't hold me up anymore and sweat dripped off my nose.

Janie lay on the bed, same as always. At least she hadn't cried for close to twenty-four hours.

I hopped in the shower, head tipped back into the spray.

Her depression threatened to bring mine back. That, along with my blue balls had me on edge.

Fuck it. Time to move.

Imagining her tight cunt wrapped around my cock had me swelled and leaking in a matter of seconds. Jaw clenched, I took myself in hand with a glob of her conditioner and jerked myself hard and fast. I bit back my groan as cum flew from my cock in thick ropes. When the last shudder rippled through me, the first spurt had long swirled away down the drain.

Somewhat relaxed, but hardly sated, I finished in the bathroom and packed up my shit, my mind fucking set.

"What are you doing?" Janie asked, pushing up to sit, her eyes wide, full of fear.

"Packing up."

"You're leaving me?" she half-shrieked, and I hurried to gather her in my arms.

"No, baby. *We* are leaving."

"But—"

"You're going to pull up your big girl panties, sit on the back of my bike, and we're going to put some miles behind us and that damn, disgusting diner I can't stand the thought of eating at again. We're going to see some countryside. Make headway toward getting home."

"Sure you still want me?" She asked the same question to leave her lips dozens of times already.

"Yes." I brushed her hair away from her face. "Now, come on. Go brush your teeth and pack up your stuff. We're heading out in a half hour."

Janie

I thought sure as shit he'd been about to leave me behind. My heart had clenched to the point of pain, and I felt myself nearing the edge of hysteria. His quick words and hug had calmed me faster than anyone had been able to, though.

Feeling like a deflated balloon wrinkled from lack of helium, I slid off the bed and forced myself to gather up my things.

Hawk had thrown a load of laundry into the office's pay machines the day before, so at least I wasn't packing dirty clothes.

He went to the office to check out while I splashed water on my face and braided my hair to hang down my back. As usual while in a low, I couldn't bring myself to look in the mirror. Depression still sat heavy enough on my shoulders. I didn't need to see the dark circles under my eyes and the paleness of the rest of my face.

"Ready?" Hawk asked when I came out of the bathroom.

I still had issues looking him full in the eye, so I busied myself lacing up my riding boots. "Sure."

Five minutes later, the bike rumbled to life, and I closed my eyes and laid my cheek on his back, actually taking an interest in his hard body and manly scent. While I didn't flush through with heat and my panties stayed dry as a bone, I took heart in the normalcy of enjoyment in something so little. Sure, on a high I'd be salivating and soaked between my thighs, but I wouldn't complain. At least *something* felt good.

We took it easy that first day back on the road, pulling into a hotel long before dinner time. The pizza Hawk had delivered to our room didn't appeal to me, but

I forced myself to chew and swallow down one slice. He smiled as though encouraged by my eating, and same as since I'd crashed, didn't try to touch me sexually when he finally crawled under the covers with me.

A couple days later, we entered New York, and my heartbeat slowed when he continued east on Route 90 rather than turn south toward where I lived. He'd been serious about taking me home with him. Even though I was fucked up in the brain and couldn't control myself, he stayed true to his word.

I didn't deserve such a man. Tears ran down my cheeks against his colors as I hugged his back, beyond thankful, even though a voice in my head constantly whispered he'd get sick of me eventually.

Twice while on the road, I'd powered up my cell phone to shoot off a quick text to Tasha and my dad, letting them know that I was doing well. I hadn't told either that I wasn't going home to New York, though. Figured I'd save that for a real phone call once we reached Hawk's home in New Hampshire.

With each passing day, my low had seemed to lighten, and when Hawk pulled up in front of his house, I felt as though I was almost back to my normal self. The darkness lay like a black oil slick in my brain, but at least I was able to see beyond it.

"Welcome home, little butterfly," Hawk said the second the bike quieted beneath us.

I climbed off and stretched my back, my gaze flitting over the ranch-style home. A few miles from the club and his shop, pale blue with black shutters. The grass needed to be cut pretty badly, but the flowerbeds below the windows appeared well tended.

"It's nice," I said, smiling over at him as he stood.

He flipped open the saddlebags. "Isn't much, but it's mine, free and clear."

My smile remained as he showed me inside, giving me a quick tour. Digger had dropped off my backpack as promised. It sat on the kitchen table.

In the small master bedroom, Hawk wrapped his arms around me from behind and rested his chin on top of my head. "I'm falling hard for you, Janie, and while I know you think I'll get sick of you and ship you off, it isn't happening."

My throat thickened, and I rested my hands on his arms.

His cock swelled against my backside, but he stepped away before I thought to wiggle a bit to let him know I actually felt like getting it on.

"Why don't you make yourself at home while I go grab our stuff? Gotta call Jonny, too, and let him know we're back."

Perfect time to make my own calls, I thought while sitting down on the edge of his queen-sized bed and watching him stride from the room. Pale gray walls, one bureau, no pictures, no artwork. A door leading to the attached bathroom.

Simplistic, just like the man himself.

I inhaled a deep breath and pulled my cell from my jean's back pocket. Tasha answered before the first ring finished.

"Finally! Where are you? How are you?" Her words tumbled out.

"I'm in New Hampshire."

I must have stunned her with the answer because it took a few seconds for her to speak again. "New Hampshire?"

"Yeah." I glanced around his—our—room again. "Hawk brought me home to his place."

"For how long?"

"Indefinite."

"Shit."

I found myself smiling again. "Right? I even crashed—hard—a couple days ago, but he says I belong with him and that's that."

"Shit," she repeated with a half-giggle. "You sound really good for having just crashed."

"Feeling somewhat better. Not quite normal, but decent enough I feel like eating and fucking again."

More laughter over the line lifted my lips higher. "Your dad is going to shit a brick."

My smile faded as her giggled words hit my ear. "How bad is it?"

"He threatened to call the cops and report you missing a few times, but I showed him your texts."

"Didn't he get the ones I sent him?"

"Yeah, but you know your dad."

I slumped, unaware I'd been strung rod-straight, and let out a breath. "Need to call him next to fill him in and see about getting some of my stuff shipped up here."

"Shit. Good luck with that one."

Yeah, and she doesn't know the half of it—nor will she or Dad for a long ass time if I can help it. "Gotta get going. I'll give you a call in a few days. Tell Lori I'll call her too once I'm settled in."

"'K."

I hung up and chewed on the inside of my lip.

Hawk came into the room with our bags and set them on the bed beside me while glancing at the phone in my hand. "Everything okay?"

"Yeah." I attempted a smile, but my twisting stomach shone through if his furrowed brow was any indication. "Gotta call my dad."

"I'll talk to him if you need me to."

"Thanks."

He left me alone, gently shutting the bedroom

door behind him.

Time to face the fire.

Heartbeat slamming in my ears, I hit the speed dial for Dad.

"Janie? Sweetheart?" he answered, half-breathless, his voice pitched higher than usual. "Tell me you're all right."

"I'm good, Dad." My voice shook the slightest bit.

"Thank Christ. I've been worried sick. The hell were you thinking running off like this with some random strange biker? Who is he? Who does he ride with?"

I'd already lied by omission, might as well protect both our asses until I couldn't any longer. "His name is Jack Richards." *Half-lie*, I told myself, trying to ease my conscious. On a high, I never would have given a shit about lying to my dad.

"Jack Richards..." Dad paused a few seconds, just long enough to kick in another burst of adrenaline to my already shaking limbs. "Don't know the name. He in a gang?"

"Just rides with some of his buddies." *Not an outright lie.*

"When are you getting home? I thought you'd be here by now from your last text."

"Yeah. About that." I stood and paced across the hardwood flooring, my free hand fisted at my hip. "He asked me to stay with him, and I agreed."

The pregnant silence that followed had me on the verge of puking.

"I crashed hard a couple days ago, Dad, but he still wants me." The words flew from my lips when I couldn't stand the silence over the line any longer. "He's generous, attentive, and crazy loyal, Dad. The type of guy every woman wants but can't ever find."

"I don't like the idea of you moving in with a man I've never met, Janie." Dad's stern voice, the one that always made me cringe, sounded loud and clear over the phone. "You've known him for what? Just over a week?"

"He's a good guy," I said, inflicting as much persuasion in my voice as I could. "Has his own motorcycle shop, his own house…"

Dad stayed silent again, and I bit my nails waiting for him to speak. A long, loud exhalation sounded before his voice. "I want to meet him."

My heart seized. "Well, we're in New Hampshire."

"Don't you need to come get your stuff? Or, are you waiting a little longer to see if he'll toss you aside like all the other assholes you've dated?"

I actually felt the blood drain from my face, but I jumped at the chance to steer the conversation away from the two meeting. "O-others?"

Dad snorted a chuckle. "I wasn't born yesterday, Janie-girl." His pet name brought tears to my eyes. "I know you, Tasha, and Lori sneak out. I know over a half-dozen guys have dropped you once they learned the truth about your illness."

I swallowed hard even though my mind started working on how he knew those things. "Sorry, Dad."

"Don't be." He sounded gruff. Rumpled, which he never did. "I've sheltered you for far too long. Guess it's time to let my little girl fly."

A tear slid down my cheek. "Thank you, Dad."

"Let me know when you're coming down here with your Jack, so I can meet him."

"Yeah." I swallowed again, my eyes drying so damn quick I had to blink. "I'll let you know."

"How'd it go?" Hawk asked when I found him in the kitchen brewing some coffee.

"Good, surprisingly."

"Just realized that we'll need to head down to your dad's soon to get your stuff since you've only got a few changes of clothes."

I shrugged and slumped at the small table he kept pushed against the wall, my body trembling from the adrenaline that had pumped through me while speaking to my dad. "Eventually, yeah. Too tired to think about it."

"Why don't you go crawl into bed and rest while I go grab something for dinner? Cupboards and fridge are pretty bare."

"Want me to go with you?"

He smiled, his hazel eyes lingering on my lips. "Only if you want to." I shrugged again, and he chuckled, turning to grab keys from a hook by the door. "Go lay down. I'll be back in a half hour."

I did as told, burying my face into Hawk's pillow and breathing in the remnants of his scent. A twinge of desire kindled between my thighs, thank God. Having gone without for so damn long, I expected Hawk would be more than willing to soothe the growing ache in my pussy.

****

Hawk brought back more than groceries. He'd stocked up on my toiletries—shampoo, conditioner, and the razors I had in my small travel kit.

"I was gonna get you some feminine things but wasn't sure what you'd need."

My head whipped up from the coffee I cradled in my hands. What man would do such a thing without even being asked? I stared.

"What?" He paused from opening the pizza

box—our dinner—he'd also grabbed on the way home.

"You were going to buy me tampons."

He nodded, his cheekbones turning a slight shade of pink. "Figured you'd probably need them."

"I don't."

His brow rose.

"IUD. No period."

"That's fucking awesome."

"Doesn't mean I won't have the monthly mood swings," I muttered while lifting my cup. "Not that I notice with my already fucked up brain."

"You're not fucked up, Janie."

Again, my gaze jerked toward his face.

Hawk placed his palms on the table across from me and leaned into my personal space. "You're fucking beautiful. Inside and out. Every inch." His rumbled words were inflected with just enough heat my pussy tingled again.

"You're too good for me."

"The fuck I am." His steady gaze dropped to my lips again. "I'm a bad man."

"Bullshit."

"I've done bad things."

"Who hasn't?"

His attention lifted to my eyes, and we stared at each other in silence. Tension rose between us, lifting the fine hairs on my arms. It'd been too long…

With a throat clearing, Hawk turned away and retrieved our pizza. "Sorry it isn't much."

"Pizza's my fav." Face warm and blood pumping, I devoured my dinner without exchanging a word with the sexy beast sitting across from me. I helped myself to a second slice and finished it before sitting back and looking at Hawk. "What?" I asked when I noticed the smirk peeking out from his beard.

"Your appetite has returned."

"In more ways than one." I gave him a saucy smirk of my own and ran my bare toes down his jean-clad shin.

Instant lust flared to life in his eyes. "What are you doing?"

"Thinking about seducing you."

"Last time we fucked, you crashed. I can't help but think it was my fault for taking you so hard."

"Thrusting your cock deep inside my ass didn't cause my depressive episode, Hawk. My crash was long overdue."

His beard twitched as though he worked his jaw, contemplating.

Realizing he needed a little nudge, I moved from my chair to the floor beside him and slid my hand up his thigh, my head tipped back to watch his face.

The heat in his eyes flared the tingles in my pussy to downright flames. "I want you, Hawk. It's been too damn long." He swallowed and nodded, and I yanked at his belt and jeans' button with trembling fingers.

He scooted his chair back and pulled his jeans mid-thigh while I hurried to yank off the leggings I'd changed into before napping.

"Fuck, have I missed you." Hawk buried his face in my neck and wrapped his arms around me as I straddled him.

I made a noise of agreement in my throat and rubbed myself against his hard length, coating him in my wetness he inspired so quickly.

My first fuck in a semi-normal state.

A tilt of my hips lined the head of his cock between my lips, and he lifted as I lowered. An easy, slick slide, the friction rolling my eyes back into my head until he bottomed out.

"Fuck," we both said at the same time, and his arms tightened around me. "No condom," he whispered against my neck, his soft beard tickling.

"IUD, remember? And I'm clean."

"Me, too. Christ, you feel so fucking good, little butterfly." He thrust against my womb.

I gasped at the pure need that raced through me in response and began rocking on his lap. One of his hands slid up my back, fisted around my braid, and yanked my head to the side. The scrape of his teeth along my neck and up to my earlobe had me squirming, nails digging into the muscles of his t-shirt-covered shoulders as he thrust in time with my rocking.

"Your cunt is so damn tight. So fucking wet." Hawk took my mouth with a groan, thrusting hard up into me, his arm wrapped around my waist lifting and lowering me in a hastening rhythm. "I'm going to come so fucking hard ... going to fill you up with my cum."

Goddamn. His words, and the idea of him shooting deep inside of me, branding me, sent tingles racing up from my toes. "I'm going to come, Hawk." Two more hard thrusts, and fireworks exploded behind my eyelids. I cried out, and Hawk continued to fuck me hard, drawing out every last tremor.

In one fluid motion, he stood, knocked his chair over, and swept our paper plates to the floor. He laid me on the table, and I wrapped my legs around his waist as he leaned over me.

"Hold on, baby."

Hands grasping my shoulders, he plowed into me over and over, slamming against my womb. My back arched on its own as I fought to get my still-throbbing clit in line with his pelvis.

Fuck. Right there. "Fuck!" I shrieked as another mind-blowing orgasm clenched every muscle in my body.

"That's it, baby. Fuck. Me. Dry." Hawk growled his words with every thrust, and his cock swelled inside of me a heartbeat before he hollered. Hot spurt after spurt coated my pussy, and I dug my heels into his ass, desperate to pull him closer, deep inside of me until our souls merged. Perhaps then, my illness would heal, making me a whole person.

One last half-thrust, and he sagged over me onto his elbows. My turn to bury my face in his neck as my emotions swarmed. Sadness, happiness, love … they all intertwined, squeezing my throat and stinging my clenched eyelids.

Hawk

A muffled sob sounded.

Fuck. I hadn't wanted to fuck her so damn hard, so damn desperate that she would fall apart on me again. I tried to pull away from her, but Janie held tight to my arms, her legs like a python around my waist.

"I—I'm okay," she whispered, her words tear-laced. "Just ... I don't know."

I pulled back my head far enough to see her face. The wetness coating her eyes made them more green than gray, and I nearly drowned in the emotion swelling in my chest. I cared about Janie so damn much, that the thought I'd hurt her made me want to punch a fucking wall, damn the sure bruised knuckled and broken fingers I'd experienced over a dozen times before.

She released her hold on my arm to smooth a hand down my whiskered cheek. "I'm okay." Another tear slid down her cheek, and I leaned down to catch it with the tip of my tongue. Her saltiness made my mouth water for more of her. The musky sweetness between her thighs. The cock-swelling tang of her tight asshole.

"You're like a drug, and I can't get enough." My voice sounded gruff. My cock remained hard, still buried deep inside of her soaked cunt. "I'm sorry."

"Don't you dare apologize again. I'm okay. Just get emotional sometimes."

"Sure you're all right?" I asked, searching her gorgeous eyes for any inkling of a lie.

Her smile wavered, but a sparkle lit in her soft gaze. "I'm overwhelmed with feelings of falling so damn hard for you ... that's good, right?"

She squeezed my cock with her inner muscles, and I clenched my jaw against the desire to fuck her again. "That's a great thing," I said, forcing myself to lift up and back out. I dropped my gaze to my cock retreating from her slick grasp. The head of my dick slipped from her velvety folds, and a pulse of cum squirted out. I grasped her knees and spread them, watching another drip of white slip from her body and slide down to coat her asshole.

"Goddamn, are you sexy," I said, my cock jumping at the sight.

Janie reached between her thighs and smeared my cum all over her cunt. I stared as she slid her fingers up and over her clit. She wiggled her ass as a soft sigh sounded. One more round about her clit, and she dipped her fingers low, rimming her cum-covered puckered hole.

"Fuck me again, Hawk." Her quiet words jerked my head up, and I realized my jaw had unhinged while watching her finger herself. "Fuck me in the ass."

Swallowing back my groan, I glanced down again to find her fingertip sliding into her rosebud.

"Fuck."

"Please," she half-groaned the word, and I moved closer, releasing my grip on one of her knees to palm my cock.

"You sure, baby?" I asked, sliding my cock up through her soaked pussy lips to gather more wetness.

She nodded, her eyes hooded, lower lip between her teeth. "Slow…"

I rubbed the head of my cock against her ass, and she let out a low hiss as I pressed forward. Once notched inside her muscle ring, I stopped and slid two fingers into her pussy and curled them, my thumb on her clit.

Janie groaned and gyrated her hips, drawing my cock another inch into her tight heat.

"Do you like my cock in your ass?"

"Yes." She gasped as I rubbed her clit and slid in

another inch. "Fuck, yes."

"Let me in, little butterfly." I pulled back while thrusting into her pussy with my fingers. "All the way," I said, slowing shoving my cum-covered cock back into her ass until my balls rested against her skin.

"Oh, my God," she whispered, her eyes fluttering open, gaze landing on my face.

Like a fucking knife to the chest, the emotion pouring from her slammed into me, and I held still, her body tight around my throbbing dick. I pulled my fingers from her pussy and sucked them clean, uncaring traces of my cum mingled with her sweetness.

She stared at my mouth, lips parted.

I gathered her up in my arms, claimed her mouth, and held her tight while gently thrusting in and out of her ass. Like a clamp, she squeezed my cock, hot and slick. Her moans captured by my lips, her breath I inhaled into my lungs as deep as possible.

I wanted to devour everything that Janie was. I wanted her deep inside of me—me deep inside of her until there was just us.

Standing in the middle of my kitchen, the sunset glinting off Janie's auburn, messy tresses around her face, I realized I'd fallen head over heels in love with her. Every inch. Every bit—the vibrant life-filled side, and the subdued side who needed someone to hold and cherish her. Unconditionally. Always.

"You're mine, Janie," I whispered against her lips and pulled back to peer into her gray-green eyes. "I'm never letting you go."

"Yes ... oh, yes." She threaded her fingers through my hair and pulled my face back down. A gentle brush of lips, and I slid my tongue inside her mouth, mimicking our slow fuck until she panted. We came together, Janie crying out my name as I buried deep inside of her body and gave her all I had to give.

****

"How's it going with your old lady?" Digger asked the second he walked into my shop. Heavy metal music blared in the background, but he'd hollered plenty loud I'd hear him.

Shaking my head, I moved to the work bench to turn the music down. "She's not my old lady."

"Bullshit. Jonny says you're fucking gone on her." Digger grinned at me, arms crossed, biceps bulging and covered in veins. He was a fucking bull. Spent more hours at the club's gym than I did. Easier, since he had one of the two apartments on the second floor, and I lived fifteen minutes outside of town.

"I'm gone on her, yeah," I admitted.

Digger grinned, but the smile didn't pretty him up one bit. Fucker had a scar from his left ear to the corner of his mouth from a knife fight he'd gotten into years earlier with one of the Silent Demons out of New York. While Digger had ended up scarred for life, the other fucker lost his. That had been the beginning of the feud between the two clubs.

"So what … she all moved in? Got your balls twisted up tight?"

"To answer the first, she will be. As for the second, she loves when I drain my balls inside of her."

"Fucker."

"At least twice a day if not more."

Digger grumbled while I chuckled and went back to work on an engine I'd promised to have rebuilt by week's end.

"What's it feel like?"

I glanced up to find his dark eyes studying me. "What?"

"Being in love."

I burst out laughing at the seriousness on his face—and not the usual pissy, don't-fucking-mess-with-me scowl.

"Don't be an asshole," he said, the dent between his brows I was all too familiar with appearing.

"Best fucking thing in the world." I grabbed a rag and wiped grease from my hands. "I'd give her anything she asked. Rob a bank. Kill a dozen people. Sell my fucking soul to the devil himself."

"Already did that."

I huffed a snort of laughter although my past sins weren't laughable. "Yeah."

Digger's scowl smoothed. "I'm jealous as shit, you know."

My brow shot up. Digger was just as fond of the club whores as I'd been not too long ago. Pussy, ass, mouth—he'd take any hole he could get, oftentimes having two girls at once or banging a chick with another brother.

"Never thought you'd ever want to settle down with one woman," I said, tossing the rag aside.

He shrugged. "Seeing Nicky when he'd come back to get his shit … seeing the same look about you." He shrugged again. "You both got something on the inside that's hard to miss. For once, your face is like a fucking book."

One of my eyebrows rose on its own as I fought not to smile at the absurdity coming from Digger's mouth. Guess I wasn't the only poetic sap at heart Fallen Glider. Digger would have been the last I'd guessed on, though.

"So, you gonna work today, or what?" I asked, hands on my hips.

"Sure. Yeah." Digger uncrossed his arms and glanced around the shop. "Tough coming back after a two-week vacation. What's your old lady up to today?"

Chuckling, I shook my head. "Work."

"She got a job already?" he asked while glancing at my Harley parked outside the opened garage door. "You let her take your fucking truck?"

"She works from home on her laptop, but I gave her my spare truck key."

"What the hell kind of work can she do from home on a computer?"

I chuckled. Fucker didn't even own a smart phone yet. "Need to get with the times, or you'll never find an old lady of your own."

"Ha!" Digger punched my arm hard enough I barely caught myself from having to step back to keep my footing. "Knew Janie was your old lady."

We got to work, and I actually smiled most of the day. Hadn't done that for months. With the unrest, brothers leaving, and just overall quietness around the club the previous couple of months, there hadn't been much to be happy about.

Janie, my little butterfly.

I needed to get a new tattoo, I thought when I walked in my kitchen door at the end of the day to find her in one of my t-shirts cooking us some dinner with the groceries I'd brought home the day before.

She flashed a smile over her shoulder from the stove, and I crowded up against her, breathing in the scent of apples from her skin and hair. "I couldn't stop thinking about you today." I ran my hands from her waist down over her hips, noting the lack of clothing beneath my shirt. "No panties?" I asked as my cock twitched.

"Nope." She stirred something in the pot that smelled like garlic and beef, but it was the thought of her sweet pussy that had my mouth watering. With a groan, I dropped to my knees, lifted the t-shirt and showed her exactly what I'd been thinking about all day.

****

"I talked to Tasha today," Janie said when I crawled onto the bed beside her and pulled her back against me.

"Everything okay?"

"Yeah." Janie blew a breath between her lips and clasped her hands over mine resting against her stomach. "She's going to send me a box of my stuff so we don't have to head to New York anytime soon, which is good since you're backed up at work."

"Jonny can wait for the engine if I need to run you home this weekend."

"No." She answered quickly and squeezed my hand. "I don't need much. Just more clothes and some personal stuff. We can plan a trip down there later when you have more time."

I nuzzled against her unbound hair and found myself relaxing into my bed more than I ever had in the past. The ranch had been mine for a few years, but having Janie with me made it feel like home rather than a place to crash and keep all my shit. "It was nice coming home to you today."

"Mmm." She squeezed my hand again. "Missed you."

"I missed you more." Smiling, I hugged her tight, wondering if my sap-fucked brain was turning to mush. Would the other Gliders at the club notice? I hadn't stopped by for my usual two beers after work, so I expected they'd give me shit when I finally chose them over Janie for an hour or two.

I suddenly understood why Nicky hadn't returned. Rather than frown or get itchy feet, I grinned. Brotherhood was supposed to come before family. Guess the fuckers who'd made up that rule hadn't loved their old ladies.

Janie rolled to face me and smoothed down my beard with her hand, a small smile on her lush lips. "I'm happy, Hawk. Like, genuinely happy for the first time since…" Tears filled her eyes.

I tucked hair behind her ear and trailed my fingertip down her collarbone until hitting the sheet lying over the swell of her left breast.

"Since before Mom passed."

Janie had only ever told me her mom had died years earlier when Janie was a teenager. It had seemed a touchy subject, so I'd left it alone. "You miss her a lot, don't you?"

She nodded and breathed deep, trying for a smile. "She was bipolar, too, but battled depression more than dealt with manic episodes. I try to remember the somewhat normal memories, you know?"

I nodded and rubbed my hand down along her sheet-covered back.

"She used to read to me some nights. I remember once she even sang me a song while rocking me. I must have been five or so." Janie's misty eyes hazed as though reliving the memory of feeling her mother's arms. Hearing her voice.

I never longed for either from the mother I'd lost. She'd never wanted me. Blamed me for wrecking her marriage to my father even though he'd assured me countless times nothing and no one could have made her happy.

Cancer had taken her, but neither my father nor I had shed a tear over her casket.

"She hung herself." Janie's whisper pulled me back damn quick.

I blinked. "Fuck. I'm sorry."

"She couldn't handle it anymore. It's the most

selfish thing a person can do, you know?" Janie didn't seem to want an answer, so I continued to hold her, waiting as she chewed the inside of her cheek. "I've been to that point once, not long after being diagnosed, thinking my life wouldn't be any different than my mom's. Meds make all the difference, though." Her brow furrowed, but she finally met my gaze. "I might have inherited her fucked up head, but I'm not her."

I kissed her forehead, her apple-scented hair tickling my nose.

"I could never inflict that kind of pain on anyone."

"Glad to hear it, 'cuz I wouldn't be able to live without you." My confession brought more tears to her eyes.

"You probably think I cry about everything—"

"I like that you express your emotions."

She snorted a laugh and shook her head. "You say that now."

"I'll say that forever."

Her smile faded, and she touched my lips with her fingertip. "Forever," she repeated. "Nothing and no *one* will ever change that."

She pressed her entire body against mine, taking my thoughts from the emphasis of *one* to the warm, willingness of her soft warmth.

Janie

I finished up my author friend's website by the end of the first week in my new home and dove into the pile of cover art sheets the indie publisher I worked for had waiting for me. While I was far from manic, my creativity had returned, and I didn't waste any time getting caught up. Every stock photo with a bare-chested, ripped man I downloaded to make the erotic romance covers reminded me of Hawk. Every bearded hottie I cropped, every hazel-eyed, sexy stare of male models turned me on.

Hawk, the poor man, joked about being my fuck toy, but I always found him hard and willing whenever I needed to feel him inside of me. Fucking while in a normal state turned out to be ten times better than fucking while manic. Sex and being present … best thing ever. My mind could focus on the feel of him, every inch sliding in and out, stretching my body to accommodate his thick cock. No erratic thoughts jumping to what I wanted or needed to do next. Satisfaction and sated bliss.

Overheated, sweating, and still trying to catch my breath, I sprawled on our bed as he stumbled to the bathroom. His ass flexed in the candles I'd lit earlier which had all but burned to nubs while we'd fucked in every position imaginable. He was a fucking stallion. Thick, hard, with stamina and the ability to come three times in a single night.

Giggling, I rolled onto my stomach and enjoyed the euphoric tingles racing through my body, muffling my hearing.

Hawk cleaned me up, same as always, before crawling under the sheet and pulling me into his arms. My heartbeat still thrummed in my ears, a small smile on my lips.

Life couldn't be any more perfect.

"Would you mind if I swing by the club tomorrow after work?"

My stomach twisted before I could give his words proper thought. Club whores. Willing mouths and holes... I'd been in Dad's club enough times to understand how things went down. I found myself tensing and tried like hell to relax.

"Your life," I finally replied since I couldn't find it in myself to answer "yes".

"Haven't been there since we got home," he said, his fingers drawing circles on my back. "Figured it'd be good to find out what's going on."

I nodded and swallowed against the swelling of my throat.

"Want to go with me?"

My head jerked back so I could see his face in the flickering candlelight. "You want me to go to the club with you?"

"Lots of old ladies do."

I found myself smiling. "So I'm your old lady, now?"

His slow grin and twinkling eyes melted my heart. "Aren't you?"

"Guess I am," I whispered.

"I love you, Janie."

My eyes burned as tears pricked, and I held his bearded cheeks between my hands. "I love you, too, Hawk. So damn much it hurts."

He squeezed me tight to his hard chest and kissed me. Explosions of light like fireworks lit behind my eyelids as they fluttered shut ... and deep inside my heart, bringing a happiness and contentment I'd never experienced before.

My new normal, I thought sometime later as

Hawk's heavy breathing let me know he slept. I smiled at the ceiling—far from manic, but flooded with joy. Such excitement usually sent me flying, so I forced my thoughts and dreams back to reality. We still needed to head south to get my stuff. Hawk and Dad still needed to meet.

Properly back on earth, but with enough anxiety to keep me up late into the night, I considered how to deal with the sure shitstorm in our future.

****

"Welcome to the club." Hawk pulled the door open and stepped back, ushering me into the Gliders' club with a hand on my lower back. Only a handful of men sat scattered throughout the large room.

It was dim, filled with the stench of cigarettes and stale booze, eighties music blasting from hidden speakers. I grimaced and raised an eyebrow at Hawk as he came alongside me.

"Yeah. That's all Jonny." He, too, grimaced. "Been trying to get him to update the music, but he's in charge."

Only two other women lounged at the bar, club whores by the look of their skimpy outfits. I followed after Hawk, never more aware of the lack of hardness lining my face like most of the women following the gangs.

"Digger." Hawk clapped a monster of a man on the shoulder, and he turned toward me. I recognized his friend from our two days on the road together. "You remember Janie."

"Hi." I smiled at the blond who looked me square in the face, keeping his gaze from roaming.

"How are ya, little butterfly?" His lopsided smirk earned a punch to his shoulder from my man. Digger snickered and swigged his beer.

Hawk motioned me to one of the stools and sat beside his friend.

The biker with the "67" tattooed on his neck behind the bar set a bottle in front of Hawk without his having asked. "What can I get you?" he asked, turning to me.

Pale blue eyes and pitch-black hair—the kind of pretty boy most girls would swoon over. Tight white t-shirt and full tatt sleeves. Pierced eyebrow and lower lip … Tasha would be all over him.

"I'll have what he's having," I said, tipping my head toward Hawk's bottle.

"Capone, this is Janie."

"How are ya, darlin'?" he asked while flipping the cap off a bottle of beer.

"Jonny here?" Hawk asked Capone.

"Yeah, but he's got company."

"The female kind?"

The pretty boy bartender dipped his head, his smirk and twinkling eyes letting us know exactly what went on behind the door to our right clearly marked "OFFICE" in all caps.

"Guess I'll give him a minute," Hawk mumbled, tipping his drink back for a long pull. "Damn that tastes good after a long day at the shop. Want a burger, Janie? Capone makes a mean one smothered with caramelized onions and mushrooms."

"Yeah, sounds good," I said, smiling at the bartender as he started toward a swinging door.

"Turn that music down while you go," Hawk raised his voice.

Capone turned a dial on the stereo beside the cash register and disappeared through the door that I figured led into a kitchen.

The hairs on my neck rose as a skitter flicked

over my skin. Someone checked me out. I gave a quick, discreet glance around and found one of the two women blatantly staring at me. Offering her a small smile didn't lessen her resting bitch face. She tossed her dirty blonde hair over her shoulder and curled her nose.

I turned back to my beer and sipped while Hawk and Digger spoke quietly, their words barely reaching my ears. Sounded as though another handful of Gliders had left the club while the bulk of them had gone on to Sturgis.

"Jonny found their colors on his desk," Digger muttered while lifting a shot glass of amber liquid.

Hawk shook his head, his brow furrowed along with downturned lips. "The fuck is this place coming to?"

"We need new blood."

"Young blood."

Digger nodded and downed his drink. "Need to make this place what it was back in the day when Nicky and Jonny's dad ruled the place."

"Those days are long gone."

"Would seem that way." Digger poured himself another shot and leaned forward to catch my gaze. "Hawk says you're from New York. Know anything about the Silent Demons?"

My heart stalled and kicked back in as a burst of adrenaline shot through my system. "H-heard of them," I managed to squeak.

Digger turned his attention back to Hawk. "I heard their president is a rat, feeding the FBI information."

"Fucking Don Taylor," Hawk muttered.

I bristled on my stool, my face flooding with heat after having drained of blood mere seconds earlier. Shifting on my stool instead of opening my mouth didn't do jack to lessen my annoyance. My dad was no snitch. He wasn't involved with the FBI or any law agency. He was known to be old school, the type of biker who would have made a name for himself back in the seventies when the Hell's Angels ruled.

Digger muttered a few more things, more gossip, probably, but I tuned their conversation out so that I wouldn't be tempted to open my mouth and ruin everything.

How the fuck was our relationship going to get past the fact my father was the president of the Gliders' arch rivals? *No fucking way...* Tears pricked my eyelids. We were fucking doomed.

Hawk

Jonny either finally got his rocks off or got sick of trying. His office door opened about twenty minutes or so after Janie and I sat down with our drinks. Hair mussed and gaze furrowing his brow, he glanced our way. He motioned me in with a tip of his head as one of the club whores scooted around him, just as mussed up as he appeared.

"You all right hanging here with Digger?" I asked Janie while sliding off the stool.

She nodded, and her shaky smile pulled my brow into a frown. "You okay?" I asked, laying a hand on her back.

"Yeah," she whispered, trying for another smile.

I nodded but didn't fully believe her. I needed to keep my time short with Jonny and get her back home in case she broke down. While I understood her emotional swings, the other guys—and the two club whores staring at her—probably wouldn't. Embarrassment was the last thing I wanted Janie to experience at my club.

I shot a glare at Shelly, the blonde who continued to stare at Janie's back, hoping she read the warning I let show on my face. She'd always wanted more than a quick fuck with me, and probably hated the fact I'd brought another woman into the club.

"Be right back, baby." I kissed the top of Janie's head and moved across the room toward Jonny.

He still scowled, scanning the room until I walked past him into the office.

"How are things?" I asked while settling into the chair across from his desk.

"Fucking shit." He slammed the door and slumped into his chair, eyes closed. "Goddamn fucking shit."

"She didn't work for ya, huh?"

"Best cock-sucker in the club, and she's leaving me frustrated. Used to love her mouth and big tits…" Jonny shook his head and met my gaze. "Three more of our newer members left while we were in Sturgis."

"Digger told me. Any idea what's going on?"

"The clubs aren't what they used to be. Guess we aren't living up to expectation. Haven't had a war, had to do away with anyone, or been involved in any bad shit for close to ten years."

The last man knocked off had been by Nicky, and while I'd taken his place as sergeant at arms, I wasn't anxious to have to perform those types of duties if needed. Digger would have my back, though. "Seems like quite a few of the older clubs are mellowing out."

Lips pursed, Jonny sat back to look at the many pictures hanging on the office walls. Past members, cross-country rides, club cookouts.

"It's a morale thing, for sure. FBI's been sniffing around again."

"Digger said Don Taylor is a snitch."

Jonny scowled at the mention of the name of our rival's leader. "Wouldn't put it past that Silent Demon prick to flap at the jaw to cover his club's ass."

Rumor had it, they'd gotten in on the sex trafficking a few other clubs across the country made money off of. Jonny, like his father before him, wouldn't put up with that sort of shit.

"What's he have on us?" I asked, settling back into my chair. "He might know we more than support New Hampshire's opioid problem, but there's no way he has names."

"I'm not so sure. Local law bagged two of our suppliers. A couple got busted up north near where Nicky settled, too."

"Think Nicky ratted them out? They're the ones who supplied his sister and niece who OD'd."

"Can't stomach that thought, so I'm leaving it alone. Shit." He scrubbed a hand down his face, his eyes weary as they settled on me. "Some days I just want to pack up my shit and head for the hills. Say fuck it all and leave the club behind."

One of my eyebrows popped up. While I'd known Jonny's weariness affected him to the point of slugging down the hard stuff, I'd never expected him to say such a thing. "You serious right now?"

"Fuck." He snorted a wry laugh, devoid of amusement. "Can't give up the club my dad started. Unless the FBI finds a reason to toss my ass in jail and no one else steps up to lead us."

A lifer ... same as me. I grinned. "You know what we need?"

"What?"

"We ought to throw a big party," I said glancing up at the picture of the two of us at our first weekend party. "See if we can't bring in those hunkered on the outside into the fold again. Rile up some trouble, bruise up some knuckles. Down a few bottles of good whiskey."

Jonny's slow nod encouraged me.

"I'll talk Digger into doing free '67' tatts," I said. "Being marked on the neck like that usually keeps members close. We need to grow that camaraderie we had when I first joined. Brotherhood and all that shit."

Jonny tapped a finger on his desk, his dark eyes seeming to consider my words. "I'll ask Capone if we can use his camp."

I outright grinned again. It'd been years since the club had headed north to the sticks for some good old-fashioned fun. Camping, booze, and whores play acting at a good gangbang. While back in the day those types of things happened for real, Jonny's dad had done away with any type of rape being acceptable behavior for a Fallen Glider. Me? The thought of sharing a tent and getting drunk on Janie sounded mighty damn fine.

"I'm in," I said.

Jonny nodded, one corner of his lips actually rising in a semi-smirk. "Send Capone in on your way out. And, keep your ears open for any shit from the fuckers down in New York."

Janie

My meds were running low, I noted a few days later, peering down at the three pills left in one of my amber bottles. No refills, either. A quick call to my doc didn't solve the problem. It'd been months since I'd seen him. He transferred me over to his secretary to make an appointment in order to get a new prescription, but I hung up before she answered.

Fuck.

I buried my head in my arms on the kitchen table and tried to breathe through the anxiety twisting my stomach. Without my meds, I would end up in the hospital again, and with things going so well with Hawk, I couldn't allow myself to lose it.

"What's wrong?"

Hawk's low voice lifted my head, and I blinked away the tears hazing my vision of him as he shut the front door behind him. A smear of grease darkened the side of his nose, his hazel eyes full of concern.

"I need to get a new prescription, and my doc won't give me one without seeing him."

"How long until you run out?"

"Three days."

"We can head down to New York tomorr—"

"No. He can't even see me until next week," I lied, the knot in my stomach rising bile up the back of my throat.

"I might be able to pull some strings. What do you need?"

I wrote down my meds and dosage and handed them to him.

"Jonny's sister suffers from bipolar, too," he said, glancing down at the sticky note. "He might be able to get you some help."

My shoulders relaxed, but the worry in my gut didn't.

"It's gonna be okay, little butterfly." Hawk grasped my jaw in his hand and peered into my eyes. "I'll take care of you. Trust me. We'll figure this out."

Tears watered the sight of him again, and I forced a nod.

He brushed his lips across mine, and I leaned into his chest as he wrapped his arms around me. A heavy sigh rippled through me, and I breathed in the scent of leather, motor oil, and exhaust that clung to his skin after a day's work in his shop. I'd never known comfort like I found in Hawk's embrace. Tender when needed, rough and demanding when filled with lust. A few ass slaps when he felt I needed a reminder of who was in charge.

"You're too good to me," I mumbled against his sweat-dampened t-shirt.

He squeezed me tighter. "You deserve better than me."

We went back and forth a few more times about who deserved what before I giggled. "I love you."

Hawk pulled back and framed my face between his hands. "Love you more."

"Doubt that."

"Come on." He stood and tugged me to my feet. "Let's clean up and go out for dinner."

"Shower?" I asked, a tingle lighting between my thighs.

"After I turn you into a hot, panting mess."

"Yes, please."

****

Turned out, the doc Jonny's sister went to for therapy owed the Gliders a favor. He fit me in the next morning, and because of the whole non-disclosure thing, I left with a brand-new prescription in hand written out for Janie Taylor. Easy to talk to, empathetic, and a great listener, he promised to get my records from New York and take over my therapy.

Crisis averted.

While the doc told me that he wouldn't tell anyone who I really was, he encouraged me to tell the truth before something happened, something that had the potential to claim lives.

Nothing I hate worse than lying. Hawk's words rang in my ears over and over, twisting my stomach into knots. I'd pretty much done nothing *but* lie since meeting him. The longing for normalcy, the happiness of a man finally accepting my broken self, made the truth that much harder to spill.

Hawk would hate me. He would send me packing, and I'd be forced to go back to New York, my heart broken, a low like I'd never known strangling the air from my lungs.

I called Tasha that afternoon while waiting for Hawk to get home.

"About fucking time," she grumbled by way of hello.

I meandered into our bedroom, intent on the bed. "Sorry I haven't called. Been busy."

"Manic busy?"

"Actually, no. This is the most normal I've felt in a long time." I lay back on our bed and closed my eyes. "Work is busy—I'm caught up from our Sturgis jaunt— and I'm keeping house for Hawk."

"Little Suzi Homemaker, huh?" Tasha laughed. "Never thought I'd see that day."

"I don't even mind scrubbing the toilet."

"Holy fuck."

I giggled, although hiding the truth from my best friend added to the guilt eating at me. "Right?"

"You sound good, Janie. Real good."

"I'm feeling the best I have in a long time. Hawk takes good care of me. Got me in to see a new doc. Keeps me on a schedule."

"You're fucking gone on him, aren't you?"

"Said the L word and everything."

"Goddamn, that was quick."

"As cheesy as it sounds, he completes me. Grounds me in a way even my dad couldn't do." The underlying shit swept over me, dissolving my smile.

"Well damn. Guess you're never coming back then, huh?"

I chewed on the inside of my lip as my eyes popped open to stare at the white, bedroom ceiling.

"Janie?"

"I'm here."

"What's up?"

Tasha always seemed to know when something bothered me. More like a sister than a best friend, I'd told her everything, every detail to ever enter my brain. Maybe being truthful with Tasha would ease my conscience a little. "If I tell you something, do you promise to keep it to yourself?"

"Shit. You have to ask me that?"

"I'm serious, Tasha."

"So am I," she shot right back without an ounce of annoyance in her voice.

"Hawk is a Fallen Glider."

"Oh, shit."

"Yeah."

Silence settled as I chewed on the inside of my lip again.

"Damnit, Janie. What the fuck am I supposed to do with that?"

"Keep it to yourself."

"Does he know who your dad is?"

I snorted. "Fuck no, and it needs to stay that way, or he'll toss me on a bus back to New York so damn quick I'll lose my shit and end up in the hospital."

"Fuck," she whispered. "This isn't good."

"I know." I clenched my eyes shut again as pain knifed my stomach. "I—I should tell him the truth, I know, but I just can't bear the thought of losing him. It's like he's a part of me, and leaving would tear me in two."

More silence, the kind that brought on tears, lingered over the line.

Tasha finally sighed. "I won't tell anyone, Janie. You know that, but you need to figure this out. Keeping the truth from him will only hurt more the longer you let it go on."

"I know," I whispered past the ache in my throat.

"If he loves you like you love him, I doubt he'll be so quick to let you go."

"We're a Romeo and Juliet disaster in real life. No way this can end well."

Tasha didn't contradict me, and when I hung up the phone a few minutes later, I didn't feel any better for having unloaded the worries clawing away at my brain.

****

Three weeks of normal, three weeks of sex that left me boneless every time, passed, and still, I kept my secret close. We packed up and headed north on Hawk's bike, off to the sticks at Capone's camp where the Gliders used to party hard back in the old days.

We had tents set up and music blasting before the second hour on site ended. The lazy, hazy smoke from a couple of campfires wafted over the grassy area, lending an acidic yet pleasant tang in the air. September had brought an Indian summer to die for. The sun hung in the sky but didn't bring the August heat that sweltered. A gentle breeze rustled the oaks and maples surrounding the meadow, but not chilly enough for a sweatshirt.

Kegs, cases of liquor, and a dozen grills littered the area … and don't forget the club whores who'd come up in a couple of vans. A handful of other old ladies had come along with their men, and although I'd chatted with them a time or two at the club, I still didn't feel as though I belonged.

I stepped out of one of the rented outhouses to find the blonde with the resting bitch face who stared at me whenever I went to the club with Hawk pressed against her. She leaned up to talk in his ear, her hand slipping down over the colors stretched over his back.

The green, plastic door slammed behind me, and I fisted my hands at my sides. She pressed her big tits against him. Hawk sidestepped, but she followed. His frown didn't deter her.

I found myself striding over the trampled grass, the "Wanted Dead or Alive" blasting from the outdoor speakers barely reaching my consciousness past the ringing in my ears. *Fucking bitch getting all up in my man's wheels.*

"Back the fuck off," I said, grabbing her arm and spinning her away from Hawk.

He chuckled, but I kept my gaze on the bitch.

"Who the fuck do you think you are?" she hissed, leaning toward me with narrowed eyes.

"Hawk's woman, and if you've got a problem with that," I said with a smile, adrenaline coursing through my limbs, "I'll gladly help you solve it." I stared, unmoving, although my body tensed, reading to flatten her out. Fuck hair-pulling and nail-clawing. Dad had taught me how to throw a punch, and I wouldn't hesitate to defend my territory.

"I was his first, you know," the bitch said with a

smirk, tilting her head and glancing up at Hawk over my shoulder.

"And I'll be his last." I returned her smile. "Now back the fuck off before I rearrange that bad nose job in the middle of your fugly face."

More snickering sounded behind me, but I didn't take my gaze off the bitch.

She attempted a stare down, but I was Don Taylor's daughter and knew how to stand strong.

Finally, she let out an exaggerated sigh. "You can keep his old ass. There's others around here he couldn't keep up with if he tried."

"Hawk 'fucking' Richards with an endless supply of cum," I reminded her of what Hawk had told me while laughing one night after coming three times. "Trust me." I leaned toward her, needing her to lament what she'd lost. "That fact hasn't changed. He's a fucking stallion, and I doubt one single man here could keep up with him and his huge cock. You go on. Try to find someone to fill his shoes, but I promise you, he'll be filling *me*. All. Night. Long."

With a flounce of her dirty blonde hair, she turned away.

Hawk palmed my ass and spun me, laughter rumbling his chest. "Goddamn, you're so fucking hot when you're pissed."

"Who the fuck is she?"

"Just a club whore. Name's Shelly."

"She touches you like that again," I said, jumping up to wrap my legs around his waist, "and I'll fucking lay her flat."

His eyes twinkled. "I don't doubt it, my feisty little butterfly. Speaking of..." He glanced over at Digger's tent beside ours. His buddy had brought along his tattooing equipment. "Been thinking I need a red butterfly right over my heart. Whatcha think?"

While I needed to get rid of the adrenaline rushing through me—preferably by a good, hard fuck—I smiled. "You'd do that?"

Hawk tucked hair behind my ear with the hand that wasn't still clamped to my ass cheek, his eyes full of love. "Been thinking about it since the morning you crashed, and I decided I wasn't letting you go no matter what."

Tears pricked my eyes, and I pulled his head down to kiss him.

"Fucking tent is right there," Digger said from beside us a few minutes into our face sucking.

I pulled back, brow raised, my blood pumping and panties soaked.

"Later," Hawk promised with another quick kiss. "I want you tattooed over my heart first."

The Fallen Gliders partied late into the night—or early morning, rather. Hawk and I stumbled to our tent once the groping and blowjobs started taking place outdoors for all to see. I'd drunk more beer than I had in a long damn time. Enjoyed myself even, getting to know two of the other Gliders' old ladies I'd never met before as we sat beside one of the campfires with our men, burning marshmallows and eating s'mores. Although both women had twenty years on me, they seemed to accept me as one of their own without the cattiness of the insecure club whores.

I crawled into our sleeping bag with a smile, and an hour later, sexually sated, sore, and still buzzed, passed out. The second night went pretty much the same, but when we returned to our tent, we found the zipper was undone and our things rifled through.

Hawk was pissed until we accounted for our belongings. The snooping, however, scared the shit out of me. I'd kept my wallet with my ID in the bottom of my bag, and although my clothing didn't appear to be disturbed, I chewed on the inside of my lip with worry until it bled.

Before he could take the matter to Jonny and possibly make me have to lie more to cover my ass, I crawled over to where he knelt by his bag, grabbed the bulge in his leathers, and pushed him back onto our sleeping bag.

I had Digger tattoo a small hawk on my right shoulder blade the next morning, had Hawk's cock deep inside of me countless times in the next two days, seeming to obliterate his memory of the "break-in", and drank way more than was healthy. I clung to his back on the way home Monday afternoon, hungover and happy.

Hawk

The weekend party had been a success on many fronts. Janie had been accepted by my peers and the old ladies who'd camped with us, the close-knit family style of club we used to enjoy appeared to be restored, and Digger had tattooed a dozen new members into the club.

I hadn't seen Jonny smile so much since we were youngsters, new to the club. He hadn't taken any whores into his tent that I'd seen, but he'd been relaxed by the end of the weekend, seemingly back to his old self.

Gliders packed the club all that week, stopping in for the old triple Bs: beer, burgers, and blowjobs. The music cranked. Brothers laughed and slapped backs, and I couldn't help but think that Janie had something to do with it all.

She'd been the one to pull me from my depressed slump. It'd been my idea to party like we had in the old days. Hell, even Jonny had thanked her for giving us both a shot of life.

My missing link. The image tattooed over my heart with her name in cursive beneath. Branded and owned, and I couldn't ask for anything more.

Saturday night, the club fucking rocked. A live, local band dominated the scene, having set up stage in the club's corner. Loud-ass drums, whining guitars—an eighties rock cover band. I danced with Janie, her curves pressed against me.

She tore it up with a couple other women, and I couldn't keep my eyes off her ass in the jeans she'd all but painted on her body. A tight, white tank top, tits pert and bouncing ... goddamn, she was too fine.

I lounged at the bar beside Jonny, toothpick between my teeth and sweating bottle of beer in my hand.

A couple new women had been welcomed in, and one clung to Jonny like a leech, her painted lips leaving smears of red and hickies on his neck. He seemed to be enjoying himself for a change.

Janie caught my gaze, her eyes flashing in the strobe lights the band had set up. Swaying her hips, arms overhead, she captured me like a siren, and I found myself shoving through the crowd to get to her, toothpick and beer left behind on the bar.

One hand on the swell of her hip, the other tangling in her hair, I yanked her against me and devoured her mouth. She rubbed against me in time with my thrusting tongue. Her breath, sweet with a hint of hops invaded my senses, making me lightheaded. Hard.

I slid my lips along her jawline to her ear. "I want to fuck you," I half-hollered and pressed my cock against her stomach.

She sagged against me, her hands grasping at the back of my colors. Peering up at me through her eyelashes, a smirk on her lips, she nodded.

I grabbed her hand and pushed my way back through the crowd, intent on the front door.

Jonny lifted his shot glass in cheers, and I dipped my head before pushing out the door. A blast of cool air licked at my skin. Fuck trying to get home. My truck would suffice.

Janie pulled up short halfway across the parking lot. "Oh fuck," she whispered with such fear, the hairs on my neck stood on end.

I glanced over my shoulder to find her focus across the street at the liquor store.

Three trucks sat side by side facing us. The doors to all three double cabs opened, and men spilled out. Men in leathers. Big, badass motherfuckers.

I recognized the tallest biker striding out front.

The one who'd given Janie a ride in Sturgis. Don Taylor, his president, walked beside him, hands fisted.

"The fuck…" My words stalled out as they crossed the road. As one, they paused on the sidewalk.

"Janie!" Taylor called. "You all right?"

She pressed up against me, and I pulled her close as thoughts crashed around in my brain.

The Silent Demons' president drew himself up and glared at me when Janie didn't answer him. "Get your fucking hands off my daughter."

Goddamn, motherfucking shit. My suspicions were right. "Janie."

"I'm sorry, Hawk," she said, her voice tear-filled as she clung to me, but I didn't take my eyes off the line of men. "I should have told you the truth from the start. I shouldn't have—"

"Your father is the leader of the fucking *Demons*." Tension hung between Taylor's men and me. A car horn honked in the distance. The club door squeaked open behind me, letting out the blasting music and laughter, and slammed shut again.

"I'm so sorry." Janie started to move away, but I held her against me. "You lied to me."

"Yes."

"You knew what would happen once the truth came out," I said without looking at her, keeping my voice low while the battle of the stares between her father and I went on.

"I got a call that you'd kidnapped my daughter."

I jerked toward Taylor. "Who the fuck called you?"

He glanced at the club behind me, and a shiver rippled down my spine. Someone inside? Demon under cover? Traitorous Glider? My blood fucking simmered, clenching my fists.

"I'm not looking for trouble," Taylor said, although his and the Demons' body language stated otherwise. At least they kept their hands where I could see them.

"He didn't take me, Dad," Janie said, her voice high-pitched and shaky. "I went with him willingly when he asked me to, just like I told you a few weeks ago. I swear to God, he didn't know who I was until just now."

The club door opened again, but no music blared.

A few of the Demons on the sidewalk shifted as footsteps sounded behind me.

Jonny pulled up on my left, Digger on my right, and dozens of other Gliders fanned out alongside us. If the Demons had shown up the previous week, the number of brothers standing beside me would have been outnumbered by our rivals. We wouldn't have stood a chance.

"We don't want trouble, Jonny, not here, not now," Taylor said, his gaze moving to my best friend. "I'm just here to get my daughter."

"Daughter." I felt Jonny's gaze slide over me and land on Janie. "Fuck," he whispered harshly in the heavy quiet.

Even worse, someone had contacted Taylor and had lied about the situation. *A problem for another time…*

"I'm so sorry." Janie started to pull away again, and although every cell in my body screamed to keep her close, I let her loose. "I shouldn't have kept the truth from you. Both of you." Tears laced her words. "I'm sorry, Jonny, but even knowing Hawk was a rival club member, I couldn't stay away from him. Couldn't— can't—control my need for him."

Her father stared at me rather than her. While I hated the fact she'd lied to me, I couldn't let her leave.

"You don't have to go," I told her before Jonny could reply, tearing my attention from Janie's father and his men.

Tears pooled in her eyes and her lips trembled. She wrapped her arms around herself as though wanting to sink into the ground and disappear. "We were doomed from the start, Hawk."

"No."

She nodded as the tears slid down her cheeks.

"Modern day Romeo and Juliet," Digger muttered under his breath.

"A Demon's daughter and a Glider," Janie added, her voice small.

"She's got problems," Taylor said, his voice loud and clear, pulling my attention back to him.

I grit my teeth, fingernails digging into my palms. "Everyone has problems, Taylor. Your daughter has found a way to live with hers. She's strong. Resilient. I've never met a more life-filled, joyous woman in my life."

A sob sounded, breaking my fucking heart.

"You haven't seen her depressive episode I'm guessing."

"She crashed less than a week after we met."

Taylor glanced at Janie, and she nodded, still hugging herself tight less than two strides away from me. It felt like a mile.

"I love her, Taylor," I told her father, unclenching and fisting my hands again. "She belongs with me, and I'll stop anyone who tries to take her away from me."

More shifting on both sides. Tension thickened over the streetlight-lit parking lot, sending another rush of adrenaline through my blood.

"I'll do whatever it takes," I said, unmoving and ready to roll if need be.

Taylor held his own, I'll give him that. A staring match for the books between protective father and lover, our brothers standing beside us, ready for violence.

"Whatever it takes?" Taylor finally echoed my words.

I dipped my head in a single nod.

"If you love her, she comes first."

Without hesitation, I pulled off my vest and tossed it to the ground. "Always."

Digger swore beside me.

"Don't do this, Hawk," Jonny said, low enough his voice wouldn't travel.

"Gotta. Janie means everything to me." I met her gaze, the love pouring from her wet eyes slamming me in the chest. "Everything."

She swiped at the tears on her cheeks, retrieved my colors, and handed them to me. "Put it back on. Now," she said, her voice steadying. I hesitated, and she slapped the vest to my chest, all trace of sorrow gone from her beautiful face. "Now, Hawk." Fire glinted in her eyes, same as when she'd told off the club whore, Shelly.

Biting back a smirk, I took my vest from her, and she spun toward her father, hands on her hips. "How dare you ask that of him?" she all but spit the words out. "This man has been nothing but kind to me. Loving. He's helped keep me grounded over the past couple of weeks, and I've never experienced such a normal before."

"He only took you to get back at the Demons for—"

"Oh, give me a break, Dad. Someone fed you that kidnapping lie, plain and simple."

"Janie—"

"If you pursue any type of charges against him, I'll spill it all, Dad. Everything you keep in that bottom drawer of your desk. Every dirty little secret."

He stilled, eyes narrowing as he studied her face. By the set of her shoulders, I expected he found determination in her eyes. Not a threat, but a promise as her voice had indicated. "You wouldn't dare."

"Oh, I would. All the sick shit you're into? You deserve to be in jail, along with the rest of your brothers." She glanced back at me, the smile I'd heard in her voice lifting her lips. "Put the vest back on, Hawk." Once more, she turned toward her father while I did as she'd said. "If you love me, *you'll* let me go. I'm more than able to make my own choices. Allow me to be an adult finally. Let him love me."

Still, her father hesitated.

"If you're going to force his hand," Janie continued, "force *me* to choose, it'll be Hawk, Dad. Every day for the rest of my life, I want him. Even if it means sending every last Demon to jail."

I stepped forward and grasped her hand before Taylor could think to react, hoping like hell Jonny realized what Janie's words meant to our club.

She turned into me, pressing her face against my chest as I wrapped my arms around her. My fucking eyes burned. "She's mine," I said, glaring at her father again. "Mine to hold. Mine to protect." Even though I wanted to plant my fist into his nose, I hoped he heard the promise behind *my* words.

Silence hovered, the threat of violence still heavy in the air. "And to cherish?" her father finally asked, his shoulders lowering the slightest bit.

"Every fucking day." I didn't hesitate to answer.

Taylor lifted his chin as though trying to stare me down over his nose. "I hear a whisper of you mistreating her, I'll come back here and burn you all down."

I wanted to snort, tell him I'd love to see him

try—especially with whatever Janie held over him—but for her sake, I nodded.

Lips pursed, he, too, nodded and turned. "Let's go, boys."

A handful of them grumbled.

"The fuck, Taylor?" one of the men threw his way.

"Shut the fuck up and let's go!" Taylor shouted back, sweeping his arm toward the vehicles behind them.

"Fuck," Digger muttered from beside me, cracking his knuckles. "I was hoping to lay a few of those fuckers flat."

"They ever show up here again to try to take Janie," I said, keeping my voice low, "lay them *all* flat."

"Gladly."

"Hawk?"

I glanced over at Jonny. "We've got some shit to discuss, but not tonight."

"Tomorrow," Jonny said. "First thing." He turned his gaze on Janie and dipped his head, his acknowledgement of her letting me know he, too, recognized her loyalty to the club.

Arm around Janie, I strode toward my truck without another word, adrenaline flooding my bloodstream. My hand shook as I opened the passenger door and pulled it open for her. "Get in."

She scurried into the cab, and I slammed the door, stalking around the front of my truck, gaze on the Demons as they climbed into theirs.

A slew of emotions pulsed through me. Anger. Pride. Lust. I turned the key, my truck roaring to life. We pulled away first, and I kept her dad's entourage in my rearview as they disappeared in the opposite direction. "When we get home, we're going to have one long fucking talk," I said, barely able to keep my voice in check. "After I redden your ass for the danger you put us all in."

"I'm so sorry, Hawk."

"Sorry isn't what I need to hear right now, little butterfly."

Silence fell over the cab for the next ten minutes as I mulled over the fact someone had called Taylor. Lied. That bothered me more than the fact Janie had been keeping the truth from me. She hadn't trusted me to stick by her side.

Jonny needed to know about the snitch. *Tomorrow*, I reminded myself, glancing over at Janie. She chewed on her inner lip, arms around her waist, staring out the window.

I pulled into the driveway, cut the engine, and returned my hand to the steering wheel in a death grip. "I'm going to sit here for a few minutes to calm the fuck down. I want you kneeling over the bed, butt naked when I come in."

Janie's breath caught, and she didn't waste time hurrying out of the truck.

Every curse word I knew flew from my lips. While I didn't take well to someone lying to me—it'd given dozens of men a close-up meeting with my fists over the years—I understood why Janie had done it. But even if I had known she was Don Taylor's daughter, I still would have gone after her in Sturgis. Would have insisted she come home with me. Would have given up my colors in order to keep her.

She fucking belonged to me, but she needed to learn lies came with consequences. We'd gotten off damn easy. No bloodshed, no lives lost, when it could have been a fucking disaster in the club's parking lot.

One wrong word, one unexpected move could have brought hell crashing down.

I blew a long, slow breath between my lips and finally released my grip on the steering wheel. Damn lucky we got away so easy.

Handing in my colors wouldn't have hurt half as much as Janie thinking she couldn't trust me with the truth. We could have figured it out together.

Goddamn you, little butterfly.

The need to unleash my pent-up energy, the thought of her backside bared and waiting for my hand...

I climbed out of the truck and adjusted my swelling cock. Time to dish out Janie's punishment and teach her a lesson or two.

Janie

Goosebumps raised my skin. Every inch of me trembled. Tension twisted my insides, and I chewed on my lower lip, squeaking as the front door opened and shut. The deadbolt clicked. Keys landed on the table. Heavy footsteps sounded back the hallway, speeding my heartbeat.

I closed my eyes, every hair on my body standing on end as Hawk's presence filled the bedroom. I'd done as told and knelt with my back to him, naked and pressed against the side of the bed.

He still loves me, I told myself as my ears strained for every move he made. *But...* "Will you ever trust me again?" I whispered, eyes clenched shut, my heart slamming in my chest.

"After tonight, you *won't* ever lie to me again." The confidence in his voice tightened every muscle in my body and sent a shiver of goosebumps over my skin.

Boots thumped on the floor. Clothing rustled. *He'll guard my heart, but that doesn't mean he won't hurt me with those big, fucking palms of his.*

He sat beside me on the edge of the bed. "Over my lap," he said, his tone broking no argument. "Head on one side, legs on the other."

My ass tingled, readying for the swats he was about to dish out. Unable to look at his face, I did as told, my eyes still tightly shut.

Without a word, he let loose, his palm smacking my ass cheek, jolting me forward, and drawing a shriek from my lungs. He swatted the other before I could catch my breath.

Tears coursed down my cheeks. I sobbed. He continued to tan my hide, and I didn't try to escape. I deserved the punishment. I'd lied. Put so many lives in danger.

Hawk soothed a hand over my ass which had to be beet red. The sting of his caress settled in my pussy, and I lifted toward his touch. He swatted again, and I gave over to the pain that radiated into stinging pleasure.

For every swat, he caressed my entire backside until I squirmed in his hold, my tears gone, lips parted on pants and moans.

He cupped my pussy. "You're wet."

I made a noise of agreement and wiggled on his lap, trying to ease the ache in my clit.

He slid two fingers deep inside of my pussy. "Goddamn, your cunt is perfect." His fingers made a squishing noise as he pulled them out of my body. The sound of him licking them clean had me squirming for more.

In one fluid motion, he lifted and tossed me onto the bed.

"On your knees. Ass up."

I kissed the fucking mattress, offering my sopping pussy and aching backside. My body trembled for him. I needed to come, release the pent-up tension. Needed to feel him inside of me. Owning me. Forgiving me.

The bed dipped, and he grasped my hips. "No coming until I say so." He lined up and shoved into my swollen folds, burying himself balls deep.

"Oh, God!" I grasped at the sheets as he plowed into me over and over, sliding me along the mattress until my head pressed against the headboard. The frame banged against the wall as he slammed into me. Every grunt, every groan on his lips brought me closer, and I bit my lip to ground myself, keep my climax on hold.

"Fuck, Janie," Hawk growled, his cock swelled, and hot cum shot into me. Incoherent words came from his lips as he emptied into me, sporadic thrusts and growls enough I panted with need.

Hawk finished and pulled out, leaving me gaping. Unfulfilled. Hot and fucking bothered. I deserved ten times worse.

I stretched out my legs as he walked to the bathroom, his cum dripping from my pussy. More tears slid down my cheeks. If ever there had been a time for a depressive episode to swallow me whole, that should have been it.

But...

Hawk had handed in his colors for me. For *me*. Fucked up in the head Janie Taylor. The woman who had lied to him. Put the lives of him and his brothers in danger. I never would have expected him to do such a thing. His loyalty—love—ran deeper than I could have imagined.

Hawk wiped his cum from between my thighs with a warm, wet cloth and sat against the headboard.

I finally rolled to my side and looked at his face while curling into a fetal position, still nervous of what I would see on his face.

"You don't trust me," he said, his eyes blank, lips flat-lined.

"I do."

"If you did, you would have told me."

"I was afraid you would toss me on a bus and send me back to New York."

"I told you that you belonged to me. I told you I loved you."

I didn't know how to respond. Such declarations should have wiped away every doubt, every fear, but I'd been programed to believe the worst from the dozen or so guys who'd high-tailed it once seeing the true me.

"Thank fuck things didn't get out of hand

tonight." Hawk rubbed a hand down over his face and beard.

"I'm so sorry," I whispered yet again.

"Come here." He reached for me, and I crawled onto his lap, sitting sideways, my ass stinging as it rested against his thigh. He pressed my cheek to his hard chest, right atop the butterfly Digger had inked over his heart. "Do you believe me when I say that I love you?"

Unable to speak, I nodded.

"Do you believe me when I say that you're mine to hold and protect?"

Again, I nodded.

"I'm never letting you go, Janie. Never."

"You would have handed in your colors for me."

"If that's what it would have taken to protect you and my brothers, yes." He paused a moment as I again considered the lengths he'd have gone to keep me. "And you would have spilled your father's secrets to stay."

"Without a second thought," I whispered. Hawk loved me, same as I loved him, transcending brotherhood—and blood. More damn tears slid down and onto his heated skin.

Hawk angled me to face him, grasping my cheeks in his calloused palms. "Look at me."

I lifted my eyes and bit my lip against the sobs wanting to rise.

"I'd do anything for you, little butterfly. Anything to keep you by my side. Safe. Happy. And knowing you'd do the same for me..." He kissed me, gentle and slow, and I soaked in the love of every caress of his lips, every slide of his tongue.

My need flared to life again, and I weaseled my way to straddle his lap, hands between us, desperate to harden his cock again. He groaned into my mouth, his hold on my face tightening as I stroked him.

"I need you, Hawk," I whispered against his lips, coaxing him to swell in my hand.

His fingers tangled in my hair, pulling, twisting as he devoured my mouth.

"Please." I gasped against his bruising lips as he worked his hips, hardening in my grasp. A lift of my hips notched his cock inside of me.

"No more lies, little butterfly." His hazel eyes filled with intense love, but also promise of consequences.

"No more lies," I whispered.

He thrust upward, filling my swollen pussy, hands in a vise grip on my hips.

"Oh, God..." I tilted my head back, thrusting my chest out, and he obliged my unasked request, his lips and teeth closing over a nipple. I ground myself against him, my clit rubbing against his pubic bone, my fingers holding tight to the hair on his head.

Hawk nipped with his teeth—soothed with his tongue—while I squirmed in his hold, desperate.

"Fuck me, Hawk," I whined. "Please."

He lifted and slammed me back onto his hard cock. "Every time your head tells you to doubt me—" he plowed into me again, "—you remember this. Remember my cock filling you." Another deep thrust landed him against my womb. "Claiming you."

"Yes ... fuck, yes."

"Come for me, Janie. I want your cum all over my cock." Two more thrusts. "All over my balls."

My climax hit me like a crashing wave, and I cried out Hawk's name, grinding my pussy against him, needing to be closer, overwhelmed with the need to draw him so deep inside of me that I couldn't tell where he began, where I ended.

He captured my mouth, swallowed my cries, and

pumped into me, prolonging the spasms, the euphoric tingles racing through my body.

"I fucking love you, Janie," he murmured into my mouth as I sagged in his arms. Still hard, he continued to work his hips, grinding into my sopping core. "Believe me?"

"Yes," I whispered into his sweaty neck, a smile on my lips. "But can you show me again?"

With a chuckle, he rolled, trapping me beneath his hard body. He kissed my forehead, pulled out, and slid in slow and easy while linking his hands with mine overhead. He kissed my nose and slowly fucked me. He kissed my lips, the slick glide of his cock in and out of my core tingling my toes.

There was no more need for words. No more declarations of love or apology. Just two lovers sharing and showing their dedication. Their promise of forever.

The End

www.authorlynnburke.com

LYNN BURKE

EVERNIGHT PUBLISHING ®

www.evernightpublishing.com